USA Today Bestselling Author
NIKKI LANDIS

Copyright © 2020 Nikki Landis
All Rights Reserved.
ISBN 9798810986409

No part of this publication may be reproduced, distributed, or transmitted in any form or by any means, including photocopying, recording, or other electronic or mechanical methods, without the prior written permission of the publisher, except in the case of brief quotations embodied in critical reviews and certain other noncommercial uses permitted by copyright law.

This is a work of fiction. Names, places, and incidents are products of the author's imagination or are used fictitiously and are not to be construed as real. Any resemblance to actual events, locales, organizations, or persons, living or dead, is entirely coincidental.

Cover by Mibl Art

Table of Contents

CHAPTER 1 1

CHAPTER 2 7

CHAPTER 3 15

CHAPTER 4 21

CHAPTER 5 27

CHAPTER 6 37

CHAPTER 7 47

CHAPTER 8 57

CHAPTER 9 63

CHAPTER 10 71

CHAPTER 11 77

CHAPTER 12 85

CHAPTER 13 93

CHAPTER 14 99

CHAPTER 15 107

EPILOGUE 115

NAVAJO TRANSLATION 125

SNEAK PEEK RIDIN' FOR HELL	127
SNEAK PEEK SINS OF THE FATHER	137
ABOUT THE AUTHOR	147

TAREK

A worthless half breed.
Drunken troublemaker.
Ex con.
Vengeful Prick.

I've been called all those names and much worse.
Hell, at one point or another I've lived up to them all.
My only home, my only real family is the MC.
I'd die for my brothers. I'd kill for my family.
And I'd sell my soul to keep my place in the pack.
Loyalty is everything.
The club is the only thing I've truly loved.
Until Synna.
She's the one that got away.
The only woman I've ever loved.
And now she's back, full of sass and smokin' hot.
All I want is to make things right.
But a hit on the club puts her life in danger.

It's my job to keep her safe, even if she hates me for it.

Winning Synna back and protecting her from my enemies becomes my only focus.

Maybe that's why I didn't see the betrayal until it was too late. Now I'll seek vengeance with my last breath and I'm not alone. Justice is swift, especially when you ride with the hounds of Hell.

Tarek is the first in the **Lords of Wrath MC** series of hell-raisers that fiercely protect their brothers in arms, their women, and their secrets.

Author's Note

The legend of the skin-walker has lived among the Navajo people for generations. Cursed humans who can transform into other creatures, mostly wolves, bears, and birds of prey are said to roam the earth. Many believe these evil forces are so strong that skin-walkers are tempted to remain in their animal form for too long and lose their humanity, leaving them a dangerous, bloodthirsty hybrid.

As shapeshifters, skin-walkers can transform themselves into any person they want, stealing the faces and identities of others to win the confidence of their victims. The Navajo legends say that one cannot fight evil with evil. The only way to stop a skin-walker is to learn the true identity and then to call the monster by its full name.

To this day many Navajos still believe in the legends.

And some are reluctant to face the night outdoors alone . . .

Dedication

To the Navajo people and the rich Dine' culture, traditions, and legends that inspired this story.

Therianthropy

The mythological ability of human beings to metamorphose into other animals by means of shapeshifting.

Chapter 1

Tarek

A Little Bit Off (Five Finger Death Punch)

"He's gonna run!" Ronin shouted as I bolted toward the back of the house.

He was already on the front porch with Cale, and neither of them would be fast enough to catch our bond Willard Scott before he escaped. J.D. caught up to me as I shouted for him to follow closely behind. The back door slammed shut with a bang, and I knew Willard was already on his way out of the backyard before I got there. He hopped the fence and flipped me off with a wicked grin as I ground my teeth in frustration.

"Go right!" I shouted to J.D. as I veered to the left and climbed the fence, dropping down into the alley next to the house. My boots slammed the asphalt and nearly skid on the puddles left behind from a recent rain.

"Got it!" he acknowledged with a brief salute. Kid was a smartass.

I swear that was how all of our bonds seemed to go lately.

Nobody ever came along willingly. I guess it wasn't all that surprising, considering they missed their court dates and were usually in trouble for something big. The thing was, they were only screwing the person who put up bail. Somebody had to pay, and it sure wasn't gonna be the bail bondsman.

That was where we came in. The certified bail agents like us carefully and methodically stalked the defendant until we could take them down. It wasn't always violent. Sometimes people knew they were caught, and there was nothing to do about it. Many others just kept on the run, moving from place to place, or hiding in the desert caverns. Not a way I would ever want to live.

We chased Willard through the neighborhood for about ten minutes, and then we lost him. Pissed, I stopped for a moment and decided to let my animal instincts take over. Might as well let the coyote use his sense of smell to track the bounty for me. The only downside was that I had to shift, and it was the middle of the day.

I felt the presence of Cale, Ronin, and J.D. only a few seconds later as they caught up to my location. Being one of the fastest in our group, I was usually way ahead of everyone else. Today was no exception.

The four of us shed our clothes as we hid in a dense area hidden from the rows of houses lined up and down the street. The forest edge was thick with pine, oak, and aspen trees. Juniper was scattered about, too, waving in the hot Arizona air.

It wasn't long before I was on all four paws and tracking Willard through the neighborhood. J.D. lagged behind the group as I sensed something was off with him.

Letting Ronin and Cale take the lead, I slowed down and circled back a few streets until I found J.D. naked on the ground, back in human form. He was holding his gut and mumbling under his breath.

I had no choice but to shift back too.

Our clothes weren't far, so I went back and picked them up with my teeth first and then dropped the bundle on the ground next to his side when I returned. I shifted and dressed, frowning as he stared at me with an odd expression, then laughed.

"Are you sick or something?" He better be sick, or I was gonna kick his ass.

"Nah, just messing with you."

My temper flared as I took a couple of steps in his direction. "It's not the right time, bro. We're in the middle of trying to catch this bond."

J.D. shrugged, not the least bit fazed by my frustrated and angry tone. "Ronin and Cale will catch him." His snicker was almost diabolical.

I didn't doubt that Ronin and Cale would close in fast, but something was weird about J.D., and it wasn't just today. The most peculiar feeling of foreboding settled over my skin. My coyote battled from within, wanting loose to sniff him and find out what the hell he was hiding. This wasn't the place, so I shook it off.

J.D. had been acting strange lately, but I figured he was just a little high-strung. An odd smell lingered in the air, and I couldn't quite place it. My coyote bristled.

J.D. grinned wider and chuckled.

"Would you knock it off?" He really started to irritate me. "I'm gonna go find Ronin and Cale. Meet us back at the Rock."

J.D. shrugged like he had an option to refuse. "Sure."

Spinning on my heel, I left him and followed the trail to the bond.

Ronin and Cale had Willard in custody by the time I joined them. I had to explain the situation to Ronin, who seemed more than a little pissed that J.D. was causing problems and messing around on the job. I knew he would take it to Hyde. It was out of my hands now.

I walked to my truck and slid inside, thankful that was the last bounty for the day. After dealing with J.D.'s shit and missing out on catching Willard, I was in a foul mood by the time I made it back to the agency office. J.D. was on my last nerve, and I broke a pair of handcuffs I'd just bought last week. My pepper spray busted in the heat, and now my truck smelled rancid—a rotten stroke of luck.

Sighing, I entered through the back door of *Booker Daniels Bail Bonds, LLC.* There were a few loose ends I needed to tie up before I headed back home. I just wanted to drop off some paperwork and have a quick chat with Hyde before I went on my way. We had church later, and I was definitely planning on slamming back a few beers afterward. Hell, after the week I had, I might as well get drunk.

It was quiet as I approached Hyde's office, not the routine for the bond agency office. Phones were usually ringing, and the fax machine receiving constant information. I didn't think much of it until I reached the door to Hyde's office and saw the young woman standing in the center of the room, her eyes wide and her expression full of surprise as she realized she wasn't alone.

Shocked, I stepped a few paces closer, unable to believe she was actually here.

Just as beautiful as I remembered, everything about her seemed to call out to me, slapping my senses alive with her soft perfume. Every part of my body instantly tuned in to her soft curves, long tan legs, and seductive smile that could lure a man to his death. It was that seductive and alluring. Popping out her hip, her hand planted in the curve of her waist as she sent a glare in my direction.

I guess she wasn't over the past—just my goddamn luck.

Not that it mattered.

"Synna," I breathed out, altogether overwhelmed by the knowledge that she was not only the one that got away but was now back in town. How long, I wasn't sure. I'd sure as fuck find out. And fast.

"Excuse me," she replied curtly as she ran from the office, brushing past me without making eye contact.

I couldn't help but stare at that sexy ass as I turned to watch her, a view that conjured a hundred memories and brought them rushing to the surface. Longing, regret, and frustration warred for dominance in my head. I wondered briefly if Ronin knew his sister was coming back. He sure didn't say a word about it.

Not that he would. Fucker didn't like anyone around his sister.

Of course, that was primarily targeted toward me.

I blew out a breath, suddenly flustered and pissed.

My hands clenched at my sides with irritation that she brushed me off before I could say a word. I knew I wasn't going to last the night before I tried to speak to her again. We had too much unfinished business. I had a lot I needed to say. Shit she should hear before she decided I wasn't worth speaking to and walked away forever. She would be at the bar later. Ronin would want her there, and that was my chance.

I would make my move then.

Synna Daniels was in for a rude awakening. She wasn't walking away from me twice.

Chapter 2

Synna

The Rush (JJ Wilde)

"G<small>IRL, ARE YOU SURE</small> you want to do this? Ronin isn't expecting you for another month."

Dani's whine was almost comical. Almost. Sometimes her drama was too much.

"I know, but I miss my brother. It's time I went back and visited him. There's nothing else happening on campus anyway."

She sighed, flopping down on my bed, her forlorn gaze sweeping over the last suitcase as I zipped it closed. "We've been roommates for over four years. It's going to be weird."

"Yeah, I know," I agreed, "but you can come to Flagstaff whenever you want. I've always got a place for you to crash."

Dani's lower lip stuck out. "It won't be the same."

Maybe, but I was ready to leave the university and return home.

"I need to go, babe. I haven't seen my brother in what feels like forever. We barely had a chance to talk the last time he visited."

She flopped back against the mattress with an exaggerated sigh. "I suppose I'll just have to come to Flagstaff soon."

"You better."

"I will," she promised. "Let's finish loading up your car."

Once my clunker of a vehicle was packed, I hugged Dani and promised to stay in contact. The drive was nearly four hours long from Tucson, and I enjoyed the trip, stopping only once for snacks and a quick bathroom break.

It had been a long time since I drove through the streets of Flagstaff. The distance and my old car didn't make it easy to come home often. I smiled when I entered the city. Flagstaff was as busy as ever, the summer heat and bright sunshine familiar and welcome.

My brother Ronin didn't have a clue that I was on my way home. I decided to surprise him, knowing that he would be thrilled. The last time we saw one another, he asked me to come home early, but my financial aid had paid for the apartment I shared with Dani until September, so I refused. Little did he know, I did so intentionally.

Bright black paint on the signage boasted *Booker Daniels Bail Bonds, LLC* as I parked in one of the empty spaces outside the front entrance. I knew it was improbable that my brother or any of the bail agents would be around at nearly three in the afternoon, but I figured it was worth a try. Ronin wasn't the type to sit behind a desk and push paperwork. He liked to be in the field with his bail agents.

My brother Ronin and his best friend Hyde Booker co-owned the business. They were the only two bail bondsmen. Everyone else was a CBA or Certified Bail Agent, which meant they were the bounty hunters, always out to catch the next idiot who failed to appear in court on their scheduled day.

That usually left Hyde in the office part-time and their secretary if they used one. Someone had to answer the phones and follow up with leads. I used to help with that until I left for the University of Arizona over four years ago.

My older brother never understood my decision to attend college so far away. He couldn't see beyond his own problems and the agency that demanded all of his time. Not that I blamed Ronin. His responsibilities were numerous, and I didn't fault him for doing what he deemed necessary to provide for us. Hyde and Ronin spent years building their contacts and growing their business. I was proud of my brother.

Add in the fact that they were also the president and V.P. of the most notorious motorcycle club in Arizona, and it made sense that I needed to get away for my sanity and independence. I'd grown up around the club, and as much as I loved the members and the brotherhood, it was also stifling. All of those protective alpha male personalities made it hard to date anyone, much less have any freedom. I always had a shadow.

The agency was quiet when I entered, not a soul in sight. Maybe they didn't have enough help. Shaking my head, I headed toward the office in the back. Poking my head around the doorway, I caught Hyde at his desk, frowning over a stack of papers.

"Yo, what's up, Hyde?"

"Synna?" His smile was a mile wide as he stood up. "You gonna give me a hug or what, Shortstack?"

Laughing, I couldn't help the big grin that spread across my face. "Maybe."

He crossed the room and slung his powerful arms around my back, patting me with big meaty fists. Hyde was a mammoth of a man. It was almost comical when you compared us side by side. He was well over six feet with shoulders so broad he had to turn sideways through most doorways.

I was a modest five-foot-three. This was precisely why he gave me the nickname Shortstack.

One that had stuck over the years.

"When did you get back?"

"Just now," I admitted. "I wanted to surprise Ronin."

"He'll be thrilled. He's missed you, even though he hasn't said much."

No surprise there. Ronin wasn't the touchy-feely, share your heart kind of guy. I was used to his gruff demeanor. It didn't mean he cared any less. "I missed you all. I'm glad to be home."

"He's out on a bond right now with Digger and Cale. Probably won't see him until we meet up later at the Rock."

That was no surprise either. The guys could always be found around the clubhouse in the evenings.

"You stickin' around for a bit? Home to stay?"

"Yeah."

"Good."

The bell above the front door dinged as someone entered, and Hyde squeezed once, letting me go. "Don't go anywhere. I'll be right back."

Customers always came first. I knew that and didn't have a problem with Hyde needing to work first before we caught up. My gaze swept over the back office as I perused the familiar charts, sticky notes, maps, and other information tacked up on the walls and scattered on the desk.

Hyde was a bit messy, but he knew where everything was located, down to the last paperclip. I tried to organize his office once and nearly ruined a bond recovery when he couldn't find what he needed. Since then, I left Hyde and his clutter alone. Shuffling feet caught my attention as I spun around, the words dying on my lips as I realized that it wasn't Hyde standing in the hall outside the door.

"Do you think Ronin—"

Surprise flickered briefly over the dark and handsome features of the man who stood in front of me, dressed in all black, hands clenching around his gear as our eyes met.

"Synna."

My name fell from his lips as sweet as honey. The deep timbre of his voice caused my entire body to tremble with swift longing and old memories. He took a few steps forward into the room and stopped.

Over four years had elapsed, and Tarek still had the ability to make my heart skip a beat when he entered the room. Swallowing hard, I lifted my chin in a desperate attempt to hide my shock. I didn't expect to see Tarek so soon. Foolishly, I thought he would be out in the field, and I would have more time to gather my thoughts before we were forced into conversation.

Shit.

"Excuse me," I managed to reply before catching his dark Navajo features that creased into a frown, rushing around his tall frame, and entering the main area where Hyde was discussing a bond with a potential client. I didn't say a word as I practically ran across the main office and outside, not stopping until I was inside my car and the door slammed shut. Gripping the steering wheel, I had to inhale several deep breaths before I could manage to start the ignition.

The entire trip from Tucson to Flagstaff, I made a point not to dwell on my past with Tarek Jones. His handsome features, thick long hair that fell to his waist, and all that rippling muscle did wicked things to my lady bits. At least, they used to, but that was before I left.

Long before he completely shattered my heart and ruined me for any other guy.

My heart did a funny lurch in my chest, and I shook my head, backing out of the parking lot and merging into traffic.

Coming home was supposed to be a happy event. I just graduated with honors and was more than excited to start using my degree. My parents would have been proud to know that I was planning on integrating what I learned about business and commerce into Ronin and Hyde's company.

Neither one knew I fully intended to use my knowledge to grow their client base.

That was why I hadn't told anyone I was coming home yet. Ronin and Hyde had come to my graduation, but they didn't expect my return for another month. I wanted to offer a proposal and my services. The truth was, I didn't wish Tarek to know I was coming home until I was ready.

Too late to change that now.

When I pulled up to the house that Ronin and I owned together, I couldn't resist a small smile. The place held a lot of memories, mostly good ones. What little I remembered of my parents was concentrated inside, along with the family photos and mementos that had been lovingly saved over the years. He hadn't changed much of the decor since I was little.

I slid from my car and unloaded all my bags, suitcases, and other boxes. It wasn't until I was nearly finished that I noticed the bright pink note posted on the windshield and held down by the wiper blade. Distracted by my thoughts and bumping into Tarek, I missed it entirely. Picking it up, I gasped as I read the message scrawled in scratchy black ink. Not funny. I crumpled the paper into a ball and shoved it into the front pocket of my jean shorts. The message was cryptic at best.

Leave town or else.

That was odd. Shaking my head, I didn't give it much thought. The guys in the MC were a bunch of pranksters, and it wasn't farfetched to think someone found out I was here and was already messing with me. Shrugging it off, I finished unpacking the car and went inside to shower and change. I always felt grimy after a long car ride, and I needed to relax and unwind.

Ronin wasn't home yet, and I didn't think he would arrive before the club met later. Flopping down on my bed, I yawned as my eyes began to close. If I was going to see Tarek again later, I needed a nap first.

Chapter 3

Tarek

Hurricane (I Prevail)

Synna Daniels couldn't stand to be in the same room with me for a single minute. Over four years since we parted ways, she still didn't forgive me for the past. My hands clenched at my sides as I watched her rush from the office and ran out the front door as if the place were on fire and she was afraid to burn.

Well, fuck.

Blowing out a frustrated breath, I followed her out and didn't bother interrupting Hyde. I would see him tonight when I met him and the rest of the club at Hyde's Rock. The bar belonged to Hyde and was passed down from his old man before he stepped down as pres of the Lords of Wrath.

He retired years ago, but Buzz could still be seen at the Rock almost every night. He was the closest thing I had to a father since my own was a deadbeat piece of shit that skipped town years ago. He rode away on his Harley with a middle finger to the wind and never returned.

My mother found out she was pregnant only a couple of weeks later. Never could track him down.

Tribal didn't return to Arizona. Last we heard, the sperm donor called the south his home. Not sure which state that he finally decided to drop some roots in, but it didn't matter. Tribal had never been a father, and I could give two shits where he ended up.

Sighing, I swung a leg over my bike and sank my ass onto the seat with a frown. It wasn't thoughts of Tribal that caused my irritation or foul mood. It was Synna's presence back in my life. Or lack of it, I should say. I sort of deserved her attitude, and it wasn't all that surprising, but the past was too long ago to hold onto any grudges. She obviously moved on from whatever we began four years ago, so I didn't get the nearly hostile way she narrowed her eyes or rushed from the office.

Pinching the bridge of my nose to ease the sudden pulse of pain, I could feel a headache coming on. I needed a drink. Bad.

The Rock was close by, and so was the man I loved like a father. I knew if there was anyone that I could talk to about Synna's return to Flagstaff, it was Buzz. He usually spent his afternoons parked in one of the many leather booths that ran the perimeter of the bar, slinging back a couple of beers. He enjoyed sharing stories with a few of the other retired brothers in the club—old founders who earned the right to sit back and let us do all the work.

Gliding out of the lot, I headed right for the Rock as I merged into traffic.

Hyde's Rock wasn't just a bar. Sure, the front part of the massive compound we owned was, but there was an entire upper level of the building full of rooms most of the brothers stayed in regularly.

Behind the bar was the chapel where we held church, the game room, a kitchen, more bedrooms, and a common room. The space was filled with plasma screen TVs, leather couches, a few pool tables, and a smaller bar located along the back wall. There were even a few pinball machines and a jukebox.

Buzz liked to play old tunes, but if Johnny Cash was on, there wasn't a soul who didn't know what that meant.

Buzz only played Johnny Cash when he was missing his old sweetheart, a lady named Whiskey Sue. From what I remembered, she was a badass bitch he hooked up with a few times back in the day. She had a reputation for holding her liquor, especially whiskey. Rumor had it that she could drink any man under the table, even Buzz. That sparked more than a few drunken binges and wild nights.

To hear Buzz tell it, he was never as happy as when he was with Sue or buried inside her. It all ended quite a few years back when Buzz's ex-girlfriend tried to start shit and spread a bunch of lies. Late one night, Whisky Sue downed a shot, flipped Buzz off, and strutted from the Rock, never to return. She left behind her teenage son J.D. who was already a prospect with the club.

Buzz never got over his one true love.

Johnny Cash was the result. Every one of us gave Buzz a wide berth when the jukebox played any of Cash's music. I loved the old guy, though. He was tough, rugged, and didn't hesitate to say what he was thinking—the kind of guy that would give you the shirt off his back or his last cigarette.

Hyde was just like him. The pair were so much alike that they even walked, laughed, and talked shit the same. Maybe that was why he was family to me as much as his old man.

Buzz was more than the retired pres of our MC. He was a father figure to nearly all of us younger patches and a solid brother to the rest. The man was a natural leader. He loved the brotherhood and the MC, and there wasn't a single damn thing he wouldn't do for any of us. That was why I knew I could head over, and he would hear what I had to say.

Buzz seemed to be waiting for me when I walked inside the bar, pulling off my leather gloves and shoving them in my back pocket. I didn't waste time but slid into the booth across from where he was seated.

Buzz sat back, leveling me with one of his signature stares. The calm gray color of his eyes could be as hard as steel when he was pissed but right now seemed like a morning mist floating above the hot desert sand. He lifted a thick arm and draped it across the back of the leather seat.

"Synna's back."

He stated the obvious right away, and it shouldn't be surprising that Hyde had already texted his old man when he saw me riding out.

"Seems that way," I stated, tempted to fidget in my seat. That unnerving gaze was still as intimidating as when I was a little kid. "She didn't bother saying a word to confirm or deny it."

"You mean she ran as soon as she saw you," he stated with humor.

I blew out a heavy breath, failing to see his amusement with the situation. "She hates me."

He chuckled lightly. "Love and hate aren't that far apart, Tarek."

"Right." I shook my head. "She's never gonna forgive me."

"Well, by rights, she has a good reason."

I didn't need the reminder. "It was for her benefit."

"Don't think she saw it that way, then, or now."

He had a point. "She deserves to have a better life. Synna never wanted to stay in Flagstaff or put down roots in Arizona. I didn't want to make her feel obligated. My life is here. The rez, my mother's hogan, my people. This is my land. It's in my blood."

Buzz knew all of this already. He nodded. We had the conversation many times in the past. "You're Navajo. She's white. It's complicated. That ain't never gonna change, son. As long as you live, you're both gonna be who you are."

A beer was placed in front of me, and I didn't bother to look up at the muffler bunny who placed it on the table.

Twisting off the cap, I downed half the bottle deep in thought.

"I'm not what she wants."

Even after all this time apart, I knew I still felt strongly for Synna. She burrowed her way under my skin long ago. Years before I understood what it meant to love a woman, months before I realized that my feelings went far deeper than friendship. For the last four years, I'd done everything I could to erase her from my memory, but my heart just wouldn't let go.

That was probably more the fault of my unique DNA. I was a shifter. A man who could transform into a beast as easily as he could walk on two feet. The whole MC was like that. A hodgepodge of loners, drifters, and outcasts that found their way to one another in the hot desert of Arizona. We all came from different nationalities, origins, and backgrounds but were united in our ability to shapeshift.

Buzz welcomed nomads and prospects. Hyde's Rock was a haven for any man who loved his Harley, freedom, and the ability to live life on his own terms.

The Lords of Wrath was established because of the vast number of shifters out there without a place to call home. A club to understand their needs and a refuge from a society that condemned and persecuted those who were different. Our rage stemmed from the secrecy we were forced into, and not many understood the pressure or toll on those who could transform into beasts.

None of this knowledge helped my current predicament.

My coyote knew Synna was his mate. He recognized her as his female one hot summer nearly a decade prior. I spent the next few years denying those feelings, and I still regretted the lost time. Only six months before she left for college did I finally act on impulse and kiss her. That kiss sealed my fate and hers.

I wanted to claim her. Ronin refused.

A shitstorm followed.

We were broken apart by fate, left devastated by the events that changed the course of our lives forever.

Synna Daniels was never gonna be mine. The sooner I accepted it, the better.

Chapter 4

Tarek

Last Time I Say Sorry (Kane Brown & John Legend)

THE SUN HAD SET by the time I finished my conversation with Buzz. Most of the club had arrived, and my brothers were drinking, playing pool, or dragging an ol' lady or club girl into their laps. Every face was familiar.

Our group was both selective and small. Had to be that way. We couldn't allow our secrets to be exposed to the world, and we didn't take chances. Those in this room had pledged their lives and loyalty to this MC, and no one betrayed the Lords of Wrath or risked severe retribution.

Oddly enough, the only person who didn't know the club's secrets was Synna. She knew nothing of the MC's true identity. Ronin insisted that we never revealed our abilities to her, and they had never been. There was only one mistake four years ago. Ronin made sure Synna left town quickly as a result. Even the club girls weren't privy to our true nature, but the ol' ladies were on a need-to-know basis, and they shared the burden.

Bitterness still lingered in my heart from that night so long ago. If things had been different, I might be with Synna now. It was a hard pill to swallow.

My thoughts were interrupted by Ronin's booming voice as he stood, pushing a blonde off his lap so fast she hit her bottom on the hardwood floor. He glanced her way and mumbled an apology, but his dark eyes lit up as he saw his sister. Both his shock and his joy were obvious.

"Synna!"

My heart nearly jumped into my throat when I saw her bright smile and the sexy sway of her hips as she practically ran to her brother. His arms wrapped around her and squeezed as she laughed, a light, tinkling, sensual sound that seemed to vibrate deep down into the pit of my stomach.

I couldn't help lifting my head a little, catching the light perfume she wore with a hint of citrus and spring flowers. My eyes closed, and I fought the urge to rush forward and tug her into my embrace. The reaction was so intense I nearly growled at her brother and had to take a few steps back or risk my coyote surging forward to stake his claim.

Not again.

Spinning around, I headed toward the bar and picked up a shot of strong liquor. I knocked back more than a few gulps of whiskey in an effort to block the way my body reacted to Synna's presence. Even with my back to the room, I could sense where she was at every moment. Whenever she moved, my senses kicked into overdrive and kept tabs on every person she spoke to, every word she said, every touch of her fingertips on everyone else's body but my own.

My coyote howled and snarled within. He was pissed. Being ignored was downright painful.

I wasn't sure how long Synna had been in the bar, but it felt like hours. Every second we were apart was total and intense agony. I winced, picking up another shot as I realized this wasn't normal. Something was off.

My protective instincts were always strong, but tonight I was on edge.

Unable to resist moving closer, I slowly made my way around the bar until we were only a few feet apart. I knew the instant she noticed my proximity because her back straightened and her shoulders pulled backward slightly. A nervous energy seemed to radiate between us.

I did the only thing I could in response.

Whispering her name so low only she would hear, I brushed my hand lightly across her elbow as I walked toward the bathrooms and the only privacy in the entire compound besides my bedroom. "Synna."

I didn't look over my shoulder to see if she followed. My senses picked up the light footsteps that proved she did. I disappeared around the corner and into an alcove that was dimly lit, the same hall only a few paces from the kitchen entrance.

My spine tingled with the knowledge that she was moving closer. I inhaled deeply when her familiar scent seemed to latch onto my body with sharp barbs, burying inside as if she were latching onto me forever and never intended to let go.

Synna nearly bumped right into me as I pulled her into my arms and held her, glancing down at that pretty face that haunted my nights. She gasped in surprise and then struggled briefly, only to relax a few seconds later like the fight was useless. It was.

We both knew it.

My heart pounded wildly in my chest, and I was sure she could feel the powerful thumps as her head rested over the spot. There was a feeling of complete and undeniable bliss that I hadn't experienced in so long that it was bitterly euphoric. I resisted the urge to scoop her up and carry her away. My breath hitching, I swallowed hard, fighting against the need to claim what was mine.

Memories of four and a half years ago assaulted my brain, but it wasn't the painful separation that surfaced. No, sweeter moments took over like the night we held one another under the stars and confessed our feelings. The vision in my mind's eyes of that night was so potent that I leaned down and pressed my lips to hers, pushing all of the longing, passion, and desire I held back into that solitary kiss.

When we finally parted, her eyes filled with tears, and my heart did a funny little stutter.

"Forgive me," I pleaded, knowing that I had to make this right between us. Whatever wrongs I had done to her, whatever mistakes I made, they weren't worth losing the connection we shared.

She blinked a couple of times as if she just now realized what was happening, and she shook her head. A single tear slid down her cheek, and I cringed. I never intended to cause her any pain.

Without giving it further thought, I lifted a finger to brush the droplet away. She lightly slapped my hand and prevented any further intimacy. My coyote howled mournfully in response, but I didn't betray my feelings. Not yet.

"It's not that easy," she whispered. "You know that, Tarek."

"You're wrong," I contradicted, holding back the urge to growl the words.

Before I could stop her, Synna ran back into the bar, and I sighed, banging my head lightly against the wall. I wasn't going to give up. Synna was back in Flagstaff, and I intended to prove to her that I was still the guy she fell in love with and swore never to leave her side.

Everything was different now. The passage of time proved neither of us was the same, and we both held onto the past.

Ronin could kiss my ass. I let him tear us apart once, but I wasn't allowing it again.

Heading back into the smoke-filled haze, I was immediately struck by a fierce and overwhelming sense of danger.

In the few seconds, it took to locate and run toward Synna, gunfire erupted outside the bar. Bullets sprayed through the glass of the windows as they shattered, scattering all over the tables, floor, and walls. Several lodged into sporadic booths or beams of wood. A couple hit flesh as screams and shouts of rage echoed in the room.

A vicious snarl left my lips as Synna cried out in terror.

The second I reached her, I threw my body in front of hers. She was pinned against the wall in the corner, but every part of her body was covered by my heavy frame. I knew I was practically crushing her, but all I could think about was preventing any of those bullets from harming my woman.

My brothers ran outside to confront the shooter, but I refused to move. I heard a few groans, more shouting, and muffled cursing. The whizz of a bullet flew right by my head and shattered the wood a few feet to my right. My body stiffened as I tried to lower Synna to the ground safely. We were far too vulnerable standing upright—an easy target for the shooter bold enough to attack the clubhouse of the Lords of Wrath.

As we moved, another bullet must have ricocheted off a metal sign or something because it grazed Synna's leg. She screamed as the crimson streak of blood rose to the surface of her skin. We hit the ground hard as I draped her with my body again, furious someone harmed her. The wound was superficial, but it would need attention as soon as I was able.

"I've got you," I promised, shielding her as I looked around the bar.

Chaos greeted me. Guns were pulled as everyone took cover, unsure if the temporary silence meant this was over or just beginning.

I knew I couldn't keep Synna here much longer. She was in too much danger. When there was a lull in the gunfire, I scooped her up and ran for the back door. I parked my bike in the back today, and I was thankful that it was the opposite lot of the one where the shooting originated.

There was no choice but to ride out fast and take Synna to safety. No way would I let her be caught in the crossfire again. I practically dragged her to the bike and gently shoved her onto the seat as I picked up a dome. She was wearing a helmet even if she tried to argue.

I was already tugging it over her head when she seemed to snap out of it and smack my hands away. "I'm not going anywhere with you, Tarek!"

"You're gonna keep this on your head and park your ass on my bike or so help me, Synna Daniels," I promised through clenched teeth, "I will spank your ass and then still make you ride in my lap!"

She must have sensed I wouldn't budge because she cursed under her breath as I swung a leg over the seat, yanked her closer, pulled her arms around my waist, and took off like all the demons from Hell were hot on my ass.

For all I knew, they probably were.

Chapter 5

Synna

Skeletons (New Years Day)

"WHERE ARE YOU TAKING me?" I shouted for the third time.

No answer. At least, nothing more than a firm squeeze of my thigh.

We kept moving further away from the city as the wind whipped around our bodies, and the cooler night air proved the late hour.

The motorcycle rumbled beneath us as I shivered and tightened my grip around Tarek's waist. I refused to acknowledge how his muscles rippled beneath his t-shirt and leather cut, demanding exploration from my traitorous fingertips. My head lowered, and I was tempted to rest it against his back. He was my savior, even if I didn't like it. Always the fierce protector.

That much hadn't changed in four long and painful years.

Despite my worry that he was the same handsome playboy as when I left, I couldn't deny there was a strong attraction between us. Everything was so easy with Tarek. In truth, it had always been that way since we were young.

As far back as I could remember, we had a unique and special friendship. There was just something about him that was irresistible. A raw, attractive power that I found hard to ignore, especially when his lips locked onto mine.

It was a mistake to linger on the kiss he dropped on me in the bar. Tarek had been drinking. I knew he wasn't thinking clearly. Caught up in the possibility of making out, he went with his instincts.

And that was the problem.

Who knew what kind of life he lived in my absence? I wasn't taking any chances. The guy probably had a girlfriend or was hooking up with a couple of the club girls always hanging around the Rock.

I had to protect my heart from Tarek Jones.

No way was I falling for his mind games. Not again.

The stars were high in the ebony sky by the time we arrived at our destination. There were no streetlights to guide our way. Only the light of the pale, silvery-white moon that kept hiding behind wisps and clusters of dark gray clouds. I had no idea where we were staying for the night.

Tempted to blurt out my questions, I waited until Tarek reached for my hand and led me into a small structure that was round in shape and seemed to squat like a careful predator watching his prey out in the dirt roads and hidden trails of the desert. Where were we?

"We're staying here tonight." Tarek didn't ask. He dictated.

Huffing out a breath, I pulled my hand from his and nearly stumbled. The interior was so dark that I couldn't see a thing.

"Maybe you should wait here." The humor and chiding tone of his voice was instantly irritating. "I'll light a few lanterns."

Wasn't there any electricity?

"There's a generator and running water, but usually, I just use the lanterns," he explained as if Tarek could read my thoughts. "Keeps the propane usage down."

"Uh, okay."

Once a few of the lanterns were lit, he placed one on a nearby kitchen table surrounded by chairs. Another was dropped on an end table next to a worn couch covered in woven tribal printed blankets. On the far side of the room, he added the third on a counter next to the sink. A row of cabinets covered most of that wall above the sink's edge. A fridge was located on the right.

An old buck stove stood in the very center, but I did see a grill pushed against another wall. Several coolers were stacked across from where I stood, along with what looked like farm equipment. There was no television but a radio perched on top of a bookcase filled with all genres of stories.

The only door was the one we entered through.

Where did people sleep?

That was when I noticed a few totes stacked to one side and what looked like an old worn dresser.

My eyes widened when I realized the entire space was one big circular room. Actually, it appeared to be an octagon.

"There's a shower and a private bed behind here."

I followed Tarek through a wall of tightly woven beads that hung to the ground. They had appeared as a wall covering, not a separation in the low lighting. A queen-sized bed, dresser, and clothing rack filled the space. Another door was off to the left. Tarek opened it, showing the shower, sink, and toilet.

"I know it's a little primitive, but this has been in my family a long time."

I nodded, unable to stop staring at the rows of wooden logs and the simple but sturdy structure. "It's a place to sleep, and that's good enough for me."

"I was hoping you'd say that. Why don't you lay down on the bed? I want to take a look at your wound."

Wound? Oh yes, I nearly forgot.

The mattress was much more comfortable than I anticipated, and I sank onto it, sighing with pleasure when I felt enveloped in a warm and soft cocoon. My eyes fluttered. The long drive from Phoenix, combined with the adrenaline rush, left my body exhausted.

As soon as I lay down at home earlier that afternoon, Dani called. My nap never happened. I yawned as Tarek pulled off my shoes and lifted my leg over his lap, sitting down at the end of the bed.

"You don't have to stay awake, Synna. I'll clean and bandage the wound carefully. It's not deep. You'll heal quickly."

His words slurred in my head as I closed my eyes, unable to fight the urge to sleep any longer.

***

THE ROOM WAS MUCH brighter when I finally opened my eyes. Sunlight trickled through the gaps in the beads and shone between the wooden blinds on the window. Tarek's voice could be heard on the other side of the bedroom as I sat up. The words were muffled, and it was apparent he was trying to stay quiet, but his frustration was clear. I slipped on my shoes and slid from the bed, making my way into the bathroom.

A couple of minutes later, I joined Tarek.

In the light of day, the structure I was in was quite a bit more shocking than last night. Painted art adorned the walls in a couple of places, and a dream catcher hung above the couch. Simple pottery lined the open cupboards and a pantry that I had missed last night next to the fridge.

The floor was hardwood, but it looked relatively new, and something told me it was probably dirt or concrete before the update. The entire place had the feeling of a cabin or vacation rental instead of a permanent residence—something to visit but not live in every day.

I stopped and stared at Tarek when I noticed what he was doing. Manipulating dough with his fingers, he tore tiny holes in cylindrical-shaped pieces of dough. Tossing the dough around his hands like a small pizza, he carefully dropped it into the hot oil on the stove. I watched as he fried the piece he finished and then placed it on paper towels to cool.

"Frybread. A Navajo tradition."

"You cook," I replied stupidly. "From scratch."

He snorted. "My mother would disagree. I'm sure she looks on with the spirits and shakes her head most of the time." He shrugged, turning his attention to another hunk of dough as he shaped, poked holes, and then fried another piece.

A pot was cooking on the stove, and the wonderful smell that accompanied it proved he had another dish for me to try. Next to it was a dark blue metal carafe that strongly smelled of coffee.

"Help yourself. There's no creamer, but I have goat's milk in the fridge and a sugar bowl on the table." He reached for a mug and placed it in my hand. "The pot has mutton stew. It's simple, but it's hearty and goes well with the bread."

It wasn't long before I enjoyed a second cup of coffee and chewed on a piece of bread, dipping it into the stew. The meal was fantastic.

"This is delicious, Tarek."

"My mother's recipe. I can't take the credit, although I watched her make it often enough when I was a small boy. She would get a kick out of watching me cook if she were still alive."

Tarek's mother passed away when he was in high school.

He was remarkably close to her, and you could still see the pain of her loss in his eyes. His Navajo roots were deep, and she was everything to him growing up. I knew he spent a lot of his time on the reservation, so it was no surprise we ended up here. I should have noticed sooner.

The conversation was minimal while we ate. As my gaze flickered over Tarek, I suddenly wanted to know all the skeletons he had buried and secrets he didn't tell anyone else. There was so much about him that I didn't know.

What kind of man was he now? Did the young guy I knew four years ago still linger behind the handsome façade of the biker who sat across from me, whose bold perusal took in every detail of my face like he was memorizing every feature?

Once Tarek had cleared the table and dishes, he sat down again with a mug of coffee and ticked his head in my direction. "I'm sure you have a few questions."

"Yeah." Plenty. "What did my brother say?" Ronin had to be freaking out.

Tarek frowned. "Ronin knows you're safe here. He didn't disagree it was best to lay low until we find out why Hyde's Rock was attacked."

That wasn't what I wanted to hear. "So, I'm on lockdown then? For how long?"

"That's undecided."

"By whose order?" I didn't think my brother would be too keen on leaving me alone with Tarek. In fact, I was surprised Ronin hadn't blown up my phone. When I checked my text messages, his only reply was brief and cryptic.

Ronin Stay with Tarek. Be safe. Love you.

I fired off a quick response.

Me This is bullshit. Love you too.

"Hyde made the final decision," Tarek answered with a note of finality.

Of course, he did. Hyde decided everything, and if he didn't, Buzz did. There wasn't a damn thing any of these guys did without permission from their president. A fact that had annoyed me for years simply because my brother and Tarek didn't seem to have a mind of their own. I didn't get it.

Didn't emergencies trump that kind of secrecy?

Whatever happened last night was big, and the fact that Tarek was keeping all the information to himself meant it wasn't going to be resolved quickly.

"I'm not a little girl anymore. You don't have to protect me from what's going on. I need to know what you find out, Tarek."

"When I have something to tell you, I will."

Pursing my lips, I shook my head. "Not good enough."

He shrugged in response, clearly agitated by the situation.

"At least tell me if anyone was injured."

"There were several brothers shot, but thankfully the wounds were superficial. Mostly everyone is fine." A tiny tick pulsed in his jaw, and that was when I noticed that he was trying to keep a tight hold on his temper.

"Mostly?"

"The shooter killed one of the prospects."

Shocked, I sat back against the seat. "Oh, God. I'm so sorry."

Tarek rose to his feet, walked briskly to the sink, and tossed in his mug. Without glancing my way, he strode toward the door. He didn't say a word until his hand was on the doorknob. Bright sunlight and scorching heat entered the moment he stepped outside.

"I'll be back in a minute. Don't worry. I'm not leaving you. Stay inside."

He shut the door before I could respond.

It was nearly two hours later before he made his way back in. Shirt slung over his glistening left shoulder; Tarek was bare from the waist up. Dirt and sweat were smeared on his upper body, clinging to the grooves and valleys that dipped between the defined muscles of his torso and chest. Each abdominal flexed as he walked, and I almost had to catch the drool that wanted to drip down my chin.

Tarek had always been handsome. The passage of time only increased the strong line of his jaw, the broad shoulders that tapered down to his narrow waist and into that perfect Adonis belt.

This man was more than just a bail agent or bounty hunter. He was a biker. My childhood friend. A Navajo Indian.

My first love.

Swallowing hard, I reached into the fridge and pulled out a cold water bottle, handing it over. In his absence, I had plenty of time to explore the small space and already knew all of the supplies stocked within. "What kind of building is this?"

"A hogan," he answered simply. "It's a sacred dwelling of my people."

Tarek never mentioned much about his heritage in the past. I knew he was half Navajo. His mother lived on the reservation until she died, part of the Navajo Nation. Tarek's father was a white man. He never knew him. His life experience was vastly different from my own. Tarek was always walking a line between his Navajo heritage and modern society, two feet in two entirely separate worlds.

"Is this your mother's hogan?"

"Yes. It's not just a shelter, but a protection, a home, and a refuge. A place to endure hardships and grow as part of the harmony between the sacred mountains under the care of "Mother Earth" and "Father Sky.""

Blinking, I wasn't sure what he meant entirely, but I understood that a hogan was special to him, especially the one we resided in.

"I never knew that much about your heritage. We didn't speak of it."

"We never had the chance," he replied bitterly, and I took a step back. He was obviously in a mood. "I'm going to take a shower."

Tarek nearly bumped into my shoulder as he rushed forward and the urge to reach out and soothe the angry beast within him was almost overwhelming. It wasn't my place to comfort him or offer anything else. Tarek and I were nothing more than two acquaintances from the past.

There were too many obstacles to hurdle to change the path we were on.

As I heard the water running and the splashing that confirmed he was occupied, my gaze swept over the hogan. Tarek's phone rested on the dining room table where he'd dropped it when he picked up the water bottle. It kept buzzing as the screen lit up.

I didn't mean to pry or sneak or put my nose in his business, but he left it there, display side up. There was no way to avoid the messages that scrolled by as I looked down.

Hyde Bones is dead.

Hyde Pick up the damn phone Tarek.

Ronin Where's Synna?

Ronin Tarek!

Ronin Tell me she's safe!

Heather Tarek, I need you.

Heather Babe?

Heather Call me back.

I wasn't pissed until I saw the last few texts.

Heather Downs. The primary reason Tarek and I never found our happy ending.

Filled with sudden anger and the familiar feeling of betrayal, I turned around as Tarek entered the room in nothing but a towel. Little dewy droplets of water clung to his upper body. He was delicious. I suddenly wanted to lick those droplets and taste his skin. Lust and desire mixed with disgust and my unexpected response.

I leveled him with a glare that probably could have knocked him to the ground if I had that kind of power. Hands clenched at my sides, I narrowed my eyes and lifted an accusing finger.

"You're still a liar."

Chapter 6

Tarek

Embrace the Rage (Message from Sylvia)

"YOU'RE STILL A LIAR."

Dumbfounded, I couldn't figure out why Synna was staring at me with such open hostility. I'd forgotten to grab a change of clothes before I hopped in the shower and was forced to enter the main room of the hogan before I could get dressed. My thoughts had been a scattered, reckless mess.

I was pissed that someone had targeted the club and was brazen enough to show up to the Rock and open fire. Synna could have died. It was bad enough that she was injured. Our newest prospect stood outside, watching the bikes out front and doing his rounds, when he was shot in the back of the head.

My brother Bones was in the hospital with severe lung and abdomen injuries. He'd been shot while covering his ol' lady and another brother who'd been shot in the leg.

It was all too much.

Who the fuck thought they could mess with the Lords of Wrath?

This shit needed to be dealt with asap.

Hyde and Buzz were pissed. Hyde's Rock was on lockdown along with the rest of the compound. Per orders, extra security was posted at the gates of the property and outside the main building. Hyde even called in a few favors, gaining additional manpower from our brother chapter in Las Vegas, Nevada.

The Nevada Lords were close with the Reapers in the Tonopah chapter of the Royal Bastards MC. Those guys were scary motherfuckers, and I was glad they were among those we considered allies.

The Royal Bastards had chapters all over the world. Their brotherhood with the Lords meant a lot to the members of our club. When we needed help, they always had our back and vice versa.

Both the Nevada clubs sent men to help with our predicament. The SAA from the RBMC was Azrael, the Angel of Death. Rael earned that nickname legit. He brought along his brother Wraith. Both guys were brawlers, sporting lots of dark ink. Wraith had a vicious set of brass knuckles he wore in any fight. Both men liked wearing black and white skull-themed makeup on their faces like it was Halloween year-round.

Rael and Wraith were on their way and hadn't reached Flagstaff yet, but I knew they would be here sometime in the next day or two. Crusher was the pres of the Nevada Lords, and he sent Bandit and Ripper. They should arrive around the same time as Rael and Wraith.

Hyde's Rock was gonna be full, and every room occupied, but none of that mattered when there was a threat against the club. Members, ol' ladies, and club girls alike were under our protection. None of us would stop until we found out who was targeting our MC and why.

Synna's safety was my top priority, in addition to helping the club find and eliminate this threat.

That was the reason I was so confused when she called me a liar. Didn't make sense at all.

"What the hell are you talking about?"

Yanking clothes from the dresser, I dropped the towel as I turned around and shoved my legs into a pair of boxers. If she got an eye full, oh well. Adding a t-shirt and jeans, I was mildly agitated when I faced her again, and she hadn't answered.

With a dainty finger pointed toward my phone, she nearly growled her next words. "Look."

I didn't bother trying to figure out why she wanted me to check my messages. Hyde and Ronin knew I had work to do if I was gonna stay on the rez. Life was more challenging here, and I had chores if Synna and I wanted food. Not to mention the fact that I needed to collect more wood.

When I looked at my cell, my heart sank. Bones was gone. He was nearly the same age as Buzz, and everyone loved him. The guy was one of the most loyal brothers I had ever known. Always had a quick smile to offer and a beer to pass around.

Fuck.

I dialed Ronin first.

"What the fuck, bro?" he shouted, clearly pissed.

"Synna is fine. She's safe. Where's Hyde?"

"Right here," he answered in the background. I was clearly on speaker.

"How's Carly?" I asked. Bones had an ol' lady named Carly, and she was a sweetheart.

"Not taking it well, Tarek. Bones is gonna be missed by everyone."

"Tanner too," Ronin added, listing the new prospect we just lost. Bones was Tanner's sponsor.

"What's the plan?" I asked, cutting straight to the point. "How long do you want me to stay on the rez with Synna?"

"As long as it takes," Ronin grumbled.

"Hey, wait a minute," Synna protested from behind me, but none of us acknowledged her outburst.

"I want a piece of this guy, Hyde. He attacked our club and hurt Synna."

"It's just a scratch," she mumbled under her breath.

"I need you with Synna, Tarek. I can't worry about her and track this fucker down at the same time." Ronin wasn't gonna budge. I could tell.

Hyde agreed. "For now. We'll text when we know something. I gotta settle this shit about Bones and Tanner. Two funerals, man." Hyde's voice was deeper than usual, and I knew he was fighting his demons and emotions. "Stay in touch."

"I will," I promised, setting down the phone with a sigh. Two brothers killed. The loss was brutal.

"Aren't you going to look at the other messages?" Synna's sarcasm was the last thing I needed.

To humor her, I picked up the cell and then cursed loudly. "Are you fuckin' kidding me? How did Heather get this number?"

Synna was looking at me with total hatred in her eyes. "Right. Like you aren't texting her. After everything that happened, how can you possibly still talk to that skank?"

If I wasn't so aggravated by everything else happening around us, I might have noticed the slight catch in her voice that betrayed her feelings. I didn't. Instead, I went from annoyed to flat out pissed, *fast*.

"Are you serious? You think you can drive back into Flagstaff and my life and question me after leaving for four years and forgetting that I even exist?"

I slammed my phone down and stalked my way in front of her, forcing her backward until her back met the wall.

"You haven't given two shits about me since the day you left. You want to judge me? Act like I owe you anything? Go for it, Synna. Just proves you haven't changed at all."

She recoiled like I had smacked her, tears filling her eyes briefly before she blinked them back. "I guess nothing really *has* changed, right? You're still selfish. You still lie and keep secrets. You still don't care about my feelings. I don't know why I expected anything different. I don't," her voice broke, and she lifted her chin, her pretty hazel eyes swimming with betrayal and pain as she continued, "I guess we have nothing more to say to one another."

Synna shoved at my chest, but I wouldn't budge. I didn't want to argue with her, and I really didn't want to rehash our past. I hated the fact that we were fighting.

Seeing the hurt in her eyes caused an ache to fill my heart. She wasn't just some girl from my past. Synna wasn't a fling.

The sexy brunette with a sweet smile and eyes that seemed to search the depths of my soul was everything to me, and I didn't want our argument to ruin the possibility of a second chance. I let my temper rule my actions instead of trying to talk about why she was so upset. My anger fizzled out as I realized I hurt her just now with my words.

Sighing, I lowered my head until we were only a few inches apart. "I didn't mean any of that. Lashing out at you was wrong."

She closed her eyes briefly and then shook her head. "That's the truth, though. We're both not over what happened in the past, and as long as that's the case, we're not ready to move forward."

As much as I didn't want to agree, she had a point. "Maybe, but—"

"I need some space, Tarek."

Reluctantly, I pulled back and allowed Synna to walk away from the conversation, but it was only temporary.

She needed a few minutes to gather her thoughts, and I wasn't such an ass that I couldn't see how deeply our disagreement, the texts from Heather, and my words affected her. I'd make it right as soon as Synna let me. If I knew anything about the woman who fled my presence, it was that she processed things in her own time, and forcing her to do anything was useless.

***

THE REST OF THE afternoon passed in silence and seemed to drag endlessly. Synna spent the entire time in the bedroom, closed off from view. I nearly barged in there a dozen times but decided it would only make things worse. My coyote kept nudging me to react, almost feral with the knowledge our mate was upset.

As much as I hated it, I gave her the space she asked for and didn't bother her.

When she finally emerged from hunger, I made dinner, but Synna still wouldn't say more than a few words. Both of us were stubborn, frustrated, and spurred on by the tension in the room. Add the fact that our sexual urges and longing seemed to linger under the surface constantly, and I was coiled tighter than a rattlesnake and ready to strike.

Only I didn't want to bite her; I wanted to give in to my desires and the need in my body. I craved her in ways that I didn't quite understand. Our argument fueled my lust, which made my coyote want to claim her even more than he already did.

The entire day was a disaster.

That night I slept on the couch as Synna returned to the bedroom. It was a long and uneasy night. I stood up and paced several times, tempted to let my coyote out and run into the desert and rocky canyons to unleash the excess energy. If there weren't a dangerous enemy on the loose, I probably would have.

The feisty look was still in her eyes the following morning. I couldn't figure out if she was mad because we argued or because I didn't join her in bed. She winced when she sat down at the table, and I realized the wound on her leg needed cleaning, and the bandage changed. I grabbed the first aid kit and set it on the table.

"Synna," I began softly, "I need to check your wound. Would you let me?"

She nodded, biting on her lower lip. I sank to my knees in front of her, lifting her leg and settling the limb over my thigh. The bandage pulled away from her skin easily, but I frowned when I saw the pink skin around the gash. There wasn't any discoloration, but it was a little warm to the touch.

"I think there's a mild infection. I'm going to clean the area, apply some ointment, and then cover it with a new bandage, but I want you to take some antibiotics and pain relievers to help the healing process."

She quirked a brow. "How did you get antibiotics? Don't you need a prescription?"

"The rez has a few doctors. It's pretty easy to get what we need and keep it on hand." She frowned in doubt. "You need to remember the reservation is home to many predators and wild animals. Snakes, spiders, scorpions, in addition to the lobo, mountain lions, and other creatures that wander onto the property. Injuries are common. There's a lot of land to cover if it's life-threatening."

Her shoulders lost some of their tension. "You're right. I didn't think of that."

Deciding it was best not to dwell on last night, I didn't bring it up. There was something else I'd rather do today. From the moment we arrived, I kept Synna hidden away in the hogan, but she was probably feeling like a prisoner by now, and fresh air and exercise would do some good.

"How about a tour of the rez?" I asked as I finished up and stored the first aid box.

She took the antibiotics and Tylenol I placed in front of her and then nodded. "As long as you feed me first."

We spent the afternoon on a long walk as I showed her all the familiar places from my youth. I caught her smile for the first time as I pointed out the sheep and goat pens. It wasn't long before we stumbled upon a group of elders sitting cross-legged around a small fire, smoking away on a pipe.

"Yá' át' ééh," I greeted.

The conversation was minimal as I dropped down and joined in, gesturing for Synna to sit. She scooted close to my side as I picked up the pipe and held it to my lips, closing my eyes as I inhaled and held the smoke until I couldn't any longer and then released it slowly, passing the pipe to her. She lifted a brow and then shrugged, taking a quick puff that made the others laugh as she blushed and passed it down.

"The pipe symbolizes peace," I explained in a whisper, keeping my voice low. "Tobacco is a sacred food to the Navajo."

She nodded, completely engrossed in watching the others as they inhaled, holding in the smoke and slowly releasing it into the air.

"The pipe ceremony is a sacred ritual for connecting physical and spiritual worlds. A link between the earth and the sky."

As I spoke, light gray smoke circled in the air and rose from the ground, surrounding the entire group in a hazy fog of euphoria and peace. I released a breath, and the tension of the last couple of days disappeared.

Drums beat a steady rhythm in the distance as a coyote's howl joined in the low voices of the spirits. Not the voice of a shifter but our animal ancestor.

I felt the presence of my mother and her clan behind me as I swayed to the beat. Words were spoken in my native tongue and echoed like a chant as I rose to my feet and began to dance. My feet padded the ground in familiar steps as my body dipped and turned, following the melody.

Flames from the fire a few feet ahead burned higher as the coyote that was my spirit animal moved to my side and lay down, resting his head on his paws. He focused on movement in the distance.

There was no danger.

I felt a swift and fierce longing fill my chest, followed by a sudden burst of love and light. Through the smoke and flames emerged the one woman I was destined to spend my life with. The female blessed by the spirits of my people.

She approached with a smile and held a small boy in her arms who couldn't have been more than two. As she passed him over, he snuggled into my embrace, his eyes the same shade as my own and hair as black as night. I swallowed hard when I realized this small child was my son.

Shocked, I lifted my gaze to the beautiful woman cradling her pregnant belly. I knew instantly that she was my wife. The love held in her gaze nearly brought me to my knees. I placed a kiss on the top of my son's head and reached for her, tugging her closer before I gazed into the hazel depths of her eyes.

"I love you, Synna."

The vision faded as I felt a rumble deep in the earth. The coyote within howled with the knowledge that our mate, future, and female that would bear our offspring was currently by my side.

Opening my eyes, I saw the nods of the elders as they realized I had a vision. Potent and undeniable, the glimpse of the future was all it took to permanently banish any doubts I had about Synna and our relationship.

I reached for her hand and lifted it, pressing a kiss on the top. When our eyes met, she inhaled a sharp breath, and I knew that she also saw the vision. Confusion, disbelief, and a hint of fear lingered in the depths. It wasn't common for those who weren't Navajo to experience what she did, but our connection was strong. The spirits knew this. I wouldn't stop proving it to her until she believed it too.

One moment could change everything.

For me, it did. Synna Daniels was *mine*.

Chapter 7

Tarek

Song #3 (Stone Sour)

Bonfires were lit as dusk fell over the rez. The elders sat in groups close to the flames and began to regale us all with old tales and the origin of our people. I listened to the stories so familiar I could recite every word from memory.

My mother used to bring me to the bonfires, and I would sit at her feet, fully engrossed in the legends and creation of our people.

Synna listened intently as one of the elders spoke, his gaze focused on the flickering flames.

"Changing Woman created the Navajo people."

"She's a Navajo deity," I interjected with a whisper. Synna slapped at my arm lightly as a hint for me to shut up, and I chuckled lightly.

"When she was about to leave on her journey back to the west, she gifted us with four clans."

"The original clans of the Navajo people are Kinyaa'áanii (The Towering House), Honágháahnii (One-walks-around), Tódich'ii'nii (Bitter Water), and Hashtł'ishnii (Mud). There are more than 100 clans among the Navajo people now."

"Wow," she whispered with awe.

"Our land is a 27,000-square-mile reservation with more than 250,000 members. The Navajo Tribe is the largest American Indian tribe in the United States." I expected her to slap me again when I said that, but she didn't. Maybe she liked facts. I could give her a few, and some were more than a little naughty.

My entire focus remained on the woman at my side. I couldn't tear my gaze away from her slightly parted lips, full and glistening in the firelight as she licked them occasionally. A smile would tug them upward every once in a while, and I almost pulled her away from the group more than once for a stolen kiss.

"Synna," I whispered as my heart pumped faster, engrossed by her beauty. Her skin glowed under the flickering flames, and I longed to caress every inch.

"Shh," she admonished.

The elder continued, "The Four Sacred Mountains are special to Navajos. Blanca to the east, Mt. Taylor to the south, the San Francisco Peaks to the west, and Mt. Hesperus to the north. We live in harmony with our Creator and with nature."

Unable to help myself, I grasped her chin and turned Synna's head in my direction, moving closer. "Navajo people view the earth as a spiritual mother. Nothing is wasted. It's the Navajo way to keep everything in balance with nature." I was ready to swoop in for a kiss when the elder began speaking of the skin-walkers.

Synna's eyes grew wide as she turned away.

"*Yee naaldlooshii* or skin-walkers are not just legends. It is not wise to go outdoors alone at night."

I reached for Synna's hand and held it as she snuggled against my side.

"Skin-walkers are cursed humans who can transform into other creatures, mostly wolves and bears, roaming the earth looking for their next victim. Evil forces take hold of these people, and they are so strong that the skin-walkers are tempted to remain in their animal form for too long. If they do, they lose their humanity. All that remains is a dangerous, bloodthirsty hybrid. A being that hunts to kill."

Synna shivered.

"Since they are shapeshifters, skin-walkers can transform themselves into any person they want. They like to steal the faces and identities of others to win the trust of their victims."

"That's awful," she replied, squeezing my arm.

"We cannot fight evil with evil. It is not the Navajo way."

I pressed a kiss to Synna's forehead, sensing her unease.

"The only way to stop a skin-walker is to learn their true identity and then call the monster by its full name."

"I'll have to remember that," she whispered.

"I don't think you'll run into one." Skin-walkers were extremely rare and not to be confused with shapeshifters like me. I was born with that ability and immune to the temptation to turn into a wicked, murdering beast.

"You never know," she disagreed.

Once the tales ended, the elders began to rise. August was the hottest and driest month of the year and perfect for a rain dance. Synna was going to be surprised when she saw us perform one.

"I'll be right back," I promised, squeezing her hand. "Don't go anywhere."

***

Synna

When Tarek returned, my jaw nearly dropped. He was the most breathtakingly beautiful man I'd ever seen, but this, seeing him dressed in the traditional garb of his people, highlighted what a truly handsome and remarkable a guy he was.

His entire appearance had changed since I last saw him. Ditching his previous clothing, Tarek was now shirtless and wearing only a pair of white cotton pants. A matching white apron cloth was draped across his hips over the material.

Deer moccasins hugged his feet, and a headband circled his head with white feathers and blue turquoise embedded in the material. I heard one of the elders say the white and blue represented wind and rain.

His long hair hung free and untied down his back. Several silver bracelets adorned his left wrist. Tribal marks and symbols were painted on his torso, chest, arms, and face. He resembled some Native American god or spirit, a powerful deity that moved with grace and strength.

I didn't know what was happening until someone mentioned it was a tradition.

The rain dance began as Tarek moved into a line formation with other men of the tribe. Men and women formed separate lines and danced in zigzag patterns, the lines moving closer together and then farther apart again.

The dance was accompanied by singing as multiple voices joined one another, overlapping but not drowning one another out. The rhythm was kept by the sound of feet hitting the ground instead of drums. I would have thought drums were used, but the dancers' footsteps were loud enough to keep the beat strong when combined with the singing.

Complicated steps were formed in a circular grid as Tarek moved. He spun around clockwise in slow circles as he kept a steady pace. His deep and sensual voice began to chant with the others and joined in the singing of his native tongue. Sometimes, he would occasionally raise his hands to the sky to urge the rain to fall.

My focus remained on his body, completely mesmerized.

Tarek moved with grace and confidence that proved he was a great warrior. Even in modern times, he was a solid member of his tribe, and it was evident he was both respected and loved.

The heat and dry air soon caused droplets of sweat to bead up on his skin. He didn't seem to notice as he continued to twist and turn to the beat, his long hair swinging lightly with every step. His chest and stomach muscles, biceps, and back bulged, and I couldn't tear my gaze from his naked upper body.

Tarek was hot as hell.

Intense desire and need rose within me, and I couldn't hide the attraction I felt, nearly crackling between us with tiny electric jolts in the summer heat. Tarek danced closer, and I could tell he wanted to be as close to me as possible. His body knew the movements so well that even when our eyes met, and he lost concentration, he never faltered or missed the beat.

In that singular, unpredictable moment when our gaze locked and the sexual tension between us sizzled, I knew he was mine, and I was his. It was the exact second when there was no going backward, no standing still in time, just moving into the future where nothing was guaranteed, but everything was right as it should be. A terrifying yet exhilarating push and pull that could only end one way.

Sweaty, skin-to-skin passion until both of us found release in one another.

It wouldn't be once. Couldn't be twice.

The only way either of us would be satisfied is if we gave in to the temptation that raged in our blood and begged for more.

I stood as he moved closer and kept dancing, twisting his body as his hands lingered close to my skin. A feral gleam entered his eyes, and the man in front of me was as much a predator as a warrior. He leaned in and captured my chin, tilting it up as his mouth hovered above my own.

"Say it."

"Kiss me," I begged, needing the connection like my next breath to survive.

Just as his lips were ready to meet mine, the first fat plops of rain began to fall. People all around us shouted and hollered with joy and excitement. The singing continued as well as dancing as the tribe celebrated the blessing of mother earth.

Everyone was distracted.

I took advantage of the moment and ran toward the hogan.

Tarek caught me outside as the rain began to fall harder. Lightning flashed above us as thunder rumbled a short distance away. The hot dirt beneath our feet sizzled as the cool rain made contact. Stars erupted above and mingled with the summer storm as the rain relentlessly soaked every inch of our bodies.

Tarek pushed me up against the outside of the hogan. Flames from a nearby bonfire were the only light source, much too far away to give detail to anyone who may look our way. There was a brief second when our eyes met, and then his lips crashed down on my own. Passion exploded between us in the damp and heated night.

Tarek's hands were roaming my body as he pushed his way between my legs. The hard bulge of his erection pressed into my stomach as I moaned with need. One of his hands gripped my ass before it slid higher and joined the other, teasing and playing with my nipples through my drenched bra.

My back arched as he pressed kisses to my throat and then trailed his hot tongue down my skin. There was a tear, and my t-shirt hit the ground after he ripped the material from my body with a guttural groan.

Damn, that was sexy.

"Need more," he growled as he sucked on the material of my bra and pushed it aside, spilling my breasts from the tight confines. Alternating between licking, teasing, and squeezing, he took total control of my body while he demanded my unconditional surrender.

"Tarek," I gasped as he lifted his head. I wouldn't deny him. It wasn't possible when my need matched what I saw in his eyes.

Reaching upward, he slid his hand behind my neck, his fingers gliding into my hair, tugging my head back as he replied, "I want you, Synna Daniels."

"Then take me," I offered with a husky tone I hardly recognized.

His tongue slid into my mouth, and I knew I was lost. Arousal ripped through my body in response, and I shivered. The warmth of his lips was such a contrast to the cool rain that continued to fall and splash onto our bodies from above that my breath exhaled on a hiss.

He tugged my hair, and I whimpered with the need to feel more of him. With another groan, he tangled his tongue with mine, then pressed kisses and nibbled down the side of my neck, pausing briefly to suckle on the sensitive spot beneath my ear. It had always been an instant turn-on, and he remembered.

I gripped the long, wet strands of his hair, holding on as he devoured me, tasting my flesh with every swipe of his tongue. There was no stopping my response. I leaned into him, licking the seam of his lips as he growled and forced his tongue back inside. I forgot everything around us but the warmth and feel of his hard body pressed to mine and the excitement racing through my veins.

He broke the kiss and made his way lower, grazing his teeth over my erect nipples. He cupped my full breasts in his hands, tweaking the peaks with his thumb and forefinger as I let out a moan of pleasure. Tarek's hips rolled into mine in response.

"I need you. Right here. Right now."

I nodded as he reached for the button on my jean shorts, and then they hit the ground as he shoved them down my thighs with my underwear. I stepped clear of the heavy, wet fabric as his pants dropped to the ground next, followed by his boxers. His cock sprang free, and I licked my lips, not at all surprised by the length and wide girth. My core pulsed with anticipation.

Tarek lifted my body as my legs wrapped around his waist. My fingers gripped the wooden exterior of the hogan and fully expected to slip due to the rain. I didn't move. He held me with an arm securely around my back and pumped his rigid length with his fist before positioning himself at my entrance and gliding inside me with a smooth thrust.

Both of us stilled.

Tarek's eyes locked on my own, and I swear the amber color deepened. "You're mine now."

I didn't deny it.

A heavy lump formed in my throat as I knew there was no other man for me other than Tarek Jones. I knew it four years ago, and I did now. Time hadn't changed a damn thing.

He began to move, pumping his hips back and forth, sliding in and out as he found a steady rhythm. My hands rose to his face, and I leaned in, capturing his lips as he continued to thrust and plunge his body into my own.

Every movement was an assault on my senses. He filled me so completely that all I could do was hold onto his shoulders and take the wild ride he was giving me. The tight knot in my core was building higher, and I knew it wouldn't be long before I came. His thrusts increased, his breath labored, and Tarek clenched my body tighter with every pump of his hips.

He was hitting deep, touching that place as only he knew how, and I was nearly undone, knowing the denial of the last four years had somehow built up this moment into an inferno neither of us could deny.

The sex was animal and needy—soul binding.

Perfect.

I cried out his name as my climax rocketed through my body seconds before he shouted out his own release.

"Synna, Synna," he rasped into my ear, his voice hoarse.

Both of us spent, he held me to his chest as if I were the most precious treasure he could possibly own. His fierce gaze held mine as his knuckles brushed against my cheek.

"What?" I whispered, unsure of the intensity that I saw.

The word had barely left my lips when he sealed his mouth over mine. He devoured my lips, licking, tasting, owning, and possessing with a feral need that was almost shocking before he pulled away so I could breathe.

Admittedly, I was a little dazed.

"I just needed one more little taste of your lips."

Tarek could have all he wanted.

We clung to each other in the rain, our bodies still wrapped around one another while neither of us moved. As I stared into his dark eyes and the flecks of amber, I knew the truth.

One moment could change everything.

For me, the intimacy we shared in the rain was the pivotal instant that cemented my commitment. Tarek's eyes glowed with that hint of honey in the dark, stormy night, and I knew I loved this man with my entire being. The past was the past. Our future was all that mattered.

Breathless, my chest heaving with the exertion of the last half hour, I whispered the words that confirmed the feelings in my heart.

"I'll never think of the rain the same."

Chapter 8

Tarek

All to Myself (Dan + Shay)

"I'll never think of the rain the same," she whispered. "Every part of tonight was beautiful."

Her words conjured an instant spark of lust when they ensnared my heart. "I'm never letting go, Synna." *I love you.*

She understood even if the words weren't spoken aloud.

I didn't expect her to say it back right away. Declaring our feelings would take a little time, but there was no doubt that I loved her, and she felt the same in return. I didn't want the words from her until she was ready, so I wouldn't push my Synna for something as important or precious until the time was right.

I scooped her up in my arms and headed inside the hogan, walking briskly until I reached the bathroom and turned on the warm water. Once it was ready, I settled her inside and then placed a kiss on her forehead.

"I'll be right back."

It only took a minute to grab our clothes from outside, and I dumped them in a basket to wash later. She was rubbing the suds of shampoo into her hair when I stepped inside the shower and stood with a grin, ogling all her curves on full display.

She was sexy as hell, and I immediately wanted to pick up where we left off, but she yawned as she rinsed out the soap, and I knew it wasn't the right time. I helped her lather a sponge and bathed her tenderly, careful to clean between her legs without being rough. As she moved out from under the spray, I stepped in quickly and washed in record time.

Once we were both clean, I grabbed a towel and dried her off first. She ran a brush through her hair as I dried off and unashamedly naked, picked her up, and settled us both beneath the covers of the big bed.

Her head rested over my heart, and I instantly remembered a night like this long ago, nearly six years prior, when we hiked out into the desert with friends and camped overnight. She stayed in my tent, cuddling next to my body as the first stirrings of desire and romantic feelings began to blossom between us.

"Remember that night?" I whispered, tugging her a little closer.

"The tent under the stars."

She didn't forget.

"Yes."

"That night was the first time I wanted you to kiss me."

Surprised, I tilted her chin up. "You did?"

"Yeah, but you didn't."

"I had no idea what I wanted back then," I admitted. Brushing her hair back, I leaned in and captured her lips in a sultry kiss. "I have no doubts now."

She smiled, her eyes fluttering. "Me either. I'm sleepy," she confessed.

Tucking her in, I rested against the pillow, content to keep her close all night. "Rest, *nizhóní.*"

***

"WHAT'S THE GAME PLAN for today?"

I made Synna breakfast and then cleared the table, sipping coffee with one arm slung across the back of her chair. "We're going on a good old-fashioned Navajo wood haul."

"A wood haul?"

"Yep," I answered, snickering at her expression. "Wood is a basic staple around the rez. Many elders can't gather on their own, so those who are able take trucks into the mountains, fill the beds with wood and then fill up the sheds for winter. August is a great time to go since the wood is dry and the ground isn't too wet. There's wild game to hunt, too, and we usually snag a few rabbits, deer, and javelina. If we're lucky, we may find a turkey."

She tilted her head to the side. "We're filling up an entire truck full of wood? Like sticks?"

Chuckling, I squeezed her shoulder and stole a quick kiss. "No, Synna, we're gathering firewood, fallen lumber, and whatever else we can find. There might be some sticks, though."

"That's a lot of wood," she observed.

"It is," I agreed. "Lots of hard work too but a great workout. We'll have help."

She still seemed a little skeptical. "I think I'll need some boots."

"You will. I can get you a pair before we leave. Watch out for ticks. They're almost always close to deer."

She shivered, clearly not liking the idea. "How long will this take?"

"We'll be gone most of the day."

An hour and a half later, we joined the group of trucks lined up at the top of the ridge. I introduced Synna to the others, and we set off into the woods to gather all the loose wood we could find. She never strayed far from my side as we made multiple trips back and forth to the truck. My stomach grumbled as I glanced at the bed and noticed it was half full.

"Hungry?"

"Definitely." Her hand rose to wipe the sweat off her brow. "It's a scorcher today."

"Sure is," I agreed, reaching for her hand and leading her to the shade. "I'll bring you something cold to drink from the cooler while I prepare lunch."

"Thanks."

The heat of a nearby fire warmed up the food I brought with us quickly. It wasn't long before I was heaping frybread, mutton, and fried potatoes onto a plate and passing it to Synna. She watched how I loaded up the bread and began eating it like a sandwich. Copying exactly, she took a huge bite, and her eyes lit up.

"This is amazing!"

Laughing at her expression, I ticked my head toward some of the other groups situated under the trees and enjoying a similar lunch. "It's a common meal on the rez. You might get sick of it."

"Never," she declared, taking another bite.

It was adorable how much she enjoyed the traditional foods of my people.

Once we finished eating, I picked up our plates and bagged the trash before resuming the wood haul. Sometime later, an eerie feeling began to tickle my senses. I felt a presence that wasn't part of our group. It was odd.

I stopped close to the nearest tree and smiled as Synna gathered more sticks, but as she turned away, I was on high alert.

Someone was watching us.

The feeling didn't leave the remainder of our time in the woods. Unsettled, I tried not to betray any worry or concern to Synna. My coyote sensed the intrusion, but I held him back, unwilling to alarm my mate. At the end of the day, we said our goodbyes to the others, and I drove back to the hogan, watching the rearview mirror the entire way.

"You know," I began as we pulled up outside, "I'm interested in your thoughts about the vision we both saw."

She blinked. "Vision?"

"Yeah, when we smoked the pipe with the elders."

"Oh, that."

Frowning, I reached for her hand. "You saw what I saw. A vision of our future together."

"A family," she whispered, tracing an invisible line on the back of my hand with her fingertip. Her head rose, and I didn't know what to make of her expression.

"Tell me what you're thinking."

"There's no guarantee that's what would happen. We can't predict the future."

"No," I assented, "but I believe strongly in the visions I see. It's not the first time I've experienced one or even the second. The spirits of my people are strong."

"I understand you feel that way. I'm just not sure that's our only option."

Swallowing hard, I felt a moment of panic. What did she mean? "Could you clarify for me, Synna? Because I *know* we're supposed to be together. It doesn't matter to me if we have two kids, ten kids, or none at all. I just know that my life won't be complete without you."

Her expression faltered, and I was surprised when tears filled her eyes. "You're something else, Tarek Jones."

"Tell me you feel it," I whispered, leaning closer.

"I do," she admitted, lifting her chin slightly. "There's no way I would deny we have a strong connection. It's just a little overwhelming."

"Then the vision doesn't matter," I conceded, pressing my lips to hers as the last word left my mouth.

"You're right," she agreed as I pulled back slightly.

Brushing my thumb over a streak of dirt on her face, I was mesmerized by her flawless features and shy, hypnotizing smile. *"Nizhóní."*

"You said that last night," she reminded me, "but I was so tired that I forgot to ask what it meant."

"Beautiful," I answered, cupping her face as my forehead rested against hers. "Simply beautiful."

Chapter 9

Tarek

Don't Let Me Go (RAIGN)

"WE BOTH NEED A shower," I observed as I led the way inside the hogan.

Synna gripped my hand tightly as I pulled her through the house and into the bathroom. Once the water was hot, I began to strip and then turned her way, easing the dirty, sweaty shirt over her head. It wasn't long before we were both naked. The sight of her glistening skin and flawless body instantly spiked my arousal.

We stepped into the water and I insisted she washed first, unable to resist lowering to my knees once she was clean. Rivulets of water trickled over her breasts and then slowly made their way down the flat contour of her belly. Her perfectly trimmed sex was only inches away.

"I want to taste you," I admitted, pushing her back gently against the wall. Lifting a leg, I placed her thigh over my shoulder as I leaned in and spread her folds apart.

"Tarek," she breathed, the fingers of her right hand threading through my damp hair.

I didn't waste time and slid my tongue into her core, loving the smoothness of her as I familiarized myself with her taste, scent, and response. Alternating between licking and sucking at her clit and using my tongue to fill her tight entrance, I slowly increased her need, bringing her to the brink of passion.

Synna uttered a slow moan and her body trembled. Her hands rose upward as she plucked and pulled at her nipples. I growled at the unashamed sight of her chasing her own pleasure, instantly turned on as my cock grew so hard it was almost painful.

Synna's hands lowered to my shoulders as her hips began to rock back and forth. I slid a finger inside her, struck by the warmth and sucking sounds as her tight pussy began to spasm.

"Tarek!" she cried out as she nearly lost her balance.

I'd never seen a sexier or more beautiful sight than the woman I was destined to marry coming apart as my fingers and tongue coaxed every last shudder from her body. Cheeks flushed, eyelashes fluttering, she nearly collapsed in my arms as I stood.

Pumping my rigid dick a few times, I was pleased when her legs spread wide and she gave me a lazy smile. Her gaze never left mine as I positioned myself at her wet core and then glided smoothly inside her with a firm thrust.

My lust and desire were so great that I had a hard time holding back and being gentle. I needed to feel her cum around my cock, and I wasn't wasting any time in getting her off again.

My lips claimed hers, my entire body aware of the heat of her skin, her slick inner walls, and the way she seemed to clutch at my arms with desperate fingers. She gripped my dick in a way no woman ever had, and my hand rose as my fingers intertwined with her own.

Pumping faster and harder, I rode the incredible high of being one with my mate. It was a wild ride as I thrust into her again and again, the steady rhythm bringing us both closer to the edge.

Synna broke the kiss as she practically wailed my name at the same time that I felt that delicious gush of fluid and the shudder of her body that proved she was coming as hard as I hoped.

My balls drew up tight and the familiar tingle in my spine let me know I was also close. A few seconds later I let myself go, spilling into Synna as I lost another part of my heart and soul to her forever.

***

EARLY THE FOLLOWING DAY, I lay in bed, waking much earlier than the lovely female snuggled against my side. My hands began to roam, my lips pressing kisses to every available inch of her skin. She was fucking irresistible, and I would never get enough.

I'd taken her hard in the shower the night before, and I was elated when she wiggled her bottom enticingly against my stomach. She wasn't too sore to go again. With a wicked grin, I pulled her backward and slid into her slick pussy as she moaned loudly.

"Morning, *nizhóní*."

"Mmmhm, Tarek."

Rocking into her slowly, I began pumping in and out as the need between us rose and began to increase. Soon I was holding her hips, pressing her belly to the mattress as I rode her hard from behind. I slammed into her wet warmth as every thrust became more intense. Her hips pushed backward and met each plunge while little sighs of pleasure fell from her lips.

Synna's fingers gripped the sheets as she cried out my name, her head tossed back as I wrapped a hand around the long strands of her hair. I knew she was close. Pumping hard and fast, I kissed her. A messy, tongue-tangling kiss that drove me wild.

Releasing her hair, I slid my free hand around her waist and rubbed a finger over her clit, pushing down before I pinched lightly. She jolted as her thighs began to shake, her orgasm soaking us both and triggering my release. A few more strokes, and I was filling her with every last drop and hoping that the vision of a son wasn't that far away.

"Synna," I groaned, completely engrossed and in love with my woman.

My mate. My future wife. The mother of my children.

I withdrew and lay on my back, immediately tugging her into my embrace. Brushing the hair back behind her ear, I made eye contact as I cradled her face in my hands.

"Ayóó Ánííníshní."

The words were spoken in my native tongue with all the conviction I had.

"What does that mean?" she whispered with awe.

"I love you."

Synna blinked, bit her lower lip, and leaned in for a kiss. For a moment, I was afraid that she wouldn't say it back or didn't want to say the words, but I was wrong. She nuzzled her nose to mine and then released a shaky breath. "I love you, Tarek Jones. I always have."

Neither of us moved until she rested her cheek over my heart, and we spent a quiet, intimate day in the hogan. I made love to her several more times, and in that few hours, only the two of us existed. No outside world. No danger. Just two lovers embracing happiness where they could find it.

***

Synna

"Tarek?" I asked, lazily drawing circles on his tanned chest. "We need to talk about something."

"Alright, sweetheart."

"Um, well," I faltered, trying to figure out a way to say what I wanted. "We haven't been using protection," I began.

"I know. I'm clean. I haven't been with anyone in a long time."

That was good. "Me either. I'm on the pill, but that doesn't mean I can't get pregnant."

He frowned, tilting my chin upward to gaze into my eyes with the fierce darkness that was uniquely Tarek. "How do you feel about children?"

"Oh, I want them," I assured him. "Not yet, though. I have a career and things I want to do before I need to stay home with babies."

He nodded, considering my words. "I can understand that. I won't deny I want a family, and I want our life together to start as soon as possible."

"You're part of a motorcycle club." I needed to get this out before he got the wrong idea. His expression was already guarded. "Your life is dangerous. The attack at the clubhouse proved that. We should wait before we think about marriage or family. There's no rush."

He sighed, closing his eyes briefly. "I don't like waiting."

"Because you're impatient," I retorted, laughing lightly.

"That's true."

Tarek slid from the bed and walked over to the dresser he'd dragged into the room the day before. Rummaging around in the top drawer, Tarek's brow furrowed.

A few seconds later, he pulled a silver object from the inside.

"I have a gift for you."

He sauntered closer with a lithe grace that was almost predatory and then spread out the silver discs in front of me that were the size of his palm.

"Wow. That's beautiful," I gushed.

"It's a concho belt. You've seen the Navajos wearing them, right?"

"Yeah, at the rain dance."

"I want you to have this one. This belt was once my mother's. It has turquoise inlaid in sterling silver. It's old but valuable."

I stood up as Tarek wrapped the exquisite belt around my waist, and the jewelry stood out against the dark blue of the t-shirt I wore. "I love it."

He smiled and then lowered his head for a leisurely and passionate kiss. "I thought you would. It's not a ring, but I'll have one of those for you soon enough."

I didn't say anything about the ring. Part of me wanted things to continue how they were, but I also knew it wasn't practical. We had lives that couldn't be put on hold forever. Instead, I kept the conversation light. "You've been spoiling me."

"Perhaps," he agreed with a wink. "You're mine to spoil."

"Maybe," I replied, teasing.

"Definitely," he argued, tugging me against his chest as he swooped in for another kiss. "I've waited long enough, Synna. We've wasted too much time." His knuckles brushed the contour of my cheek as his serious expression proved he wasn't joking. "We're together now, and that's how it's gonna stay."

My arms slipped around his neck, and I couldn't resist rising on my tiptoes and whispering in his ear, "I think you need to prove it."

When my back hit the mattress and his body covered mine, I knew we weren't leaving the room for the rest of the afternoon.

Chapter 10

Synna

Every Part of Me (Godsmack)

Tarek and I had been living in our own little bubble. Caught up in one another, we didn't think much about the outside world. The attack seemed a distant memory compared to the bliss I experienced with the man I loved, but after five days on the rez and only a few sporadic texts from my brother, I became restless.

Tarek had taken up the habit of leaving periodically, saying he had chores to do, but I noticed that he seemed on edge, almost as if something bothered him, but he didn't want to worry me, so he stayed silent.

"Tarek?"

"Yeah, sweetheart?"

"When can we leave the reservation?"

He was chopping wood from the load we brought back, and I handed over a glass of cold lemonade.

Such a normal thing to do that I nearly forgot we were hiding away from the danger outside the reservation. Tarek dropped the ax and accepted the drink but stiffened as I asked, his hand clenching the glass tightly enough that I thought it might shatter.

"I can't make that call, Synna."

Sighing in response, I didn't expect any other answer. After all, it wasn't like I didn't know how the MC worked. Ronin and Hyde had been members for as long as I could remember. Tarek was a prospect when we were young, and he patched into the club his senior year of high school. There was a specific way things went down, a hierarchy they all religiously followed. I wasn't privy to all, if any, of the decisions made.

"I know you can't tell me club business, but you have to be thinking about this too. We can't stay here forever."

"I know, *nizhóní*." Tarek placed the empty glass on the tailgate of his nearby truck and picked up my hands. "I don't want to leave the rez and safety unless it's necessary. We still don't know who attacked the club. Hyde and Ronin are doing everything they can to ensure the culprit is caught and things can go back to normal. We have plenty of connections, and help is on the way. This asshole hunting the club can't hide for long."

Arguing was pointless, especially when I couldn't change the outcome. "I hope you're right."

My phone buzzed, and I checked the screen, thrilled to see Ronin's name.

"It's about time," I answered, unable to keep the frustration out of my voice as I accepted the call. "I've barely seen or talked to you since I returned home."

"You're not exactly at the house or the Rock," Ronin replied with an attitude. "Don't be pissed at me, Syn. I'm not taking any chances with your safety. Hyde isn't either. We both know the rez is neutral ground, and there's hardly any crime. I can't bring you back into town until we find this fucker and take him down."

Pursing my lips, I made a face at Tarek, who smirked. "I understand the danger," I acknowledged, "but Tarek and I can't hide away on the rez indefinitely. I have to earn some kind of wage. Mooching isn't my style."

"I don't mind taking care of you," Tarek grumbled. His arms crossed over his chest as he narrowed his eyes, all humor disappearing. "The rez is the safest place in the entire state of Arizona."

"I agree with Tarek." Ronin evidently heard what he said.

"You two are missing the point," I complained.

"You're staying on the rez." Ronin's tone didn't leave much room for argument. Never did. Once he dictated something, that was it.

I wondered how he would feel if he knew I spent the last few days tangled up in the sheets with Tarek. "Any other orders?"

"Aw, Syn, don't bust my balls."

"Then don't be an ass." Tarek chuckled, and I shot a glare in his direction.

"Would you feel better if I came over tonight?"

"Yeah," I admitted, losing the last of my attitude. I missed my brother. Didn't he understand?

"Then I'll be there, Syn. Okay?"

"Okay, Ro."

"Hey." His voice cracked, and I knew this was hard on him too.

"Yeah?" I answered, a sudden lump in my throat.

"I love you, little sis."

"Love you back."

He ended the call, and I turned to Tarek, my relief evident. I'd felt like Ronin avoided me since this all went down, and I realized he'd just been busy doing his job as V.P. and trying to find the threat against his family. The MC was family as much as I was.

The brotherhood between the members was real. I'd seen their close friendships for many years. There was nothing the Lords of Wrath wouldn't do for one another. It was far more than just a bunch of guys wearing leather cuts and riding Harleys.

They took me in when our parents died. A car accident in the middle of the night in the rain changed our lives forever. I was shocked, too young to comprehend. Ronin was lost, too distraught to raise a child. He was ten years my senior and didn't know what to do with a little sister that needed constant supervision and care. Whiskey Sue was the one who stepped up and helped raise me with Buzz.

Ronin spent as much time with me as he could. We grew close, and it was no wonder that the Rock felt like a second home for as long as I could remember. That was true for the members of the MC too. I guess it was unavoidable that I would fall in love with a biker.

Tarek was only a few years older, but he always appeared wiser. His Navajo blood filled his veins with passion, courage, and strength that most young men didn't possess. When he became a bounty hunter, I knew it was his calling. Tarek was a warrior by blood, by birth, and by profession.

"What are you thinking about?" His voice brought me out of my musings.

"You. Me. The club." I shrugged. "It's my family as much as you and Ronin. I missed you all when I was gone. It's not fair that I'm unable to see everyone because some asshole picked a fight with the Lords of Wrath."

"I understand." His lips lifted in a slight smile as his palm rested against my cheek. *"Nídin sélį́į́ shijéí bináká hoodzą́."* Leaning in as his chest pressed closer, his lips brushed mine softly. "Missing you left a hole in my heart."

"You never told me that."

"What? That I missed you?" His hands squeezed my waist as the look on his face became serious. "I did. My heart broke the day you left."

"You told me to leave. You said you were with Heather." It was the first time I dared to say the words that completely shattered me four years prior.

"Lies." He tilted my chin up, crooking a finger underneath. "Don't you see? I'm older. I knew my path. It's been clear since I was a boy. But you, my precious Synna, were just starting your journey. I had to let you go."

Shocked, I shook my head. "No, you didn't have to do that. It tore me apart, Tarek. I thought you were in love with another girl." Tears filled my eyes, and a few slipped down my flushed cheeks.

"You would never have left otherwise. We both know that's true. The connection between us was strong then and even stronger now. I had to sever it four years ago to give you what you needed."

Chin wobbling, I nodded. He was right, even if I didn't like it. "And now?"

"Now my heart is yours. *Shijéí T'áá Hazhó'ó Niba' Iiłkił*. My heart slowly ticks for you. Only you, my Synna."

"Tarek." My lips quivered with his name in a whisper, and he closed the remaining distance between us, his mouth covering mine and dominating my senses. He kissed me with a tenderness mingled with passion as his tongue swept my mouth and tangled with my own. Raw need erupted between us as he pushed me up against the outside of the hogan.

"It's not raining, but I'm not opposed to taking you right here and now."

The words tumbled from his lips with a husky timbre, and I shivered with instant desire.

"There's no one around for miles. I need you, Synna." His lips pressed to my throat and trailed kisses and nibbles down my neck. "I need you every minute of the day."

"I need you just as much."

He lifted his head, his dark gaze smoldering. "I never stopped thinking of you the entire time you were gone. A part of me was empty without you."

I swallowed hard, overcome with emotion at his declaration.

"I'll do anything to keep you safe and protected. I know you're worried, but I've got you, *nizhóní*. Nothing will ever harm you again."

"I believe you," I promised, wrapping my legs around his waist as he picked me up. My arms slid around the taut muscles of his neck as we held one another close. "You're mine now, too, Tarek."

He growled lightly in response as his teeth nipped at my lips. "I'm going to devour you every way that I can."

"Go for it," I challenged. "Show me what you got, bad boy."

The feral gleam in his eyes shone amber as his lips curled up in a devious grin. "You better tell me to take it slow."

"No way," I teased. "I want you to lose control."

He cursed under his breath as his embrace tightened and the bulge between his legs enlarged. "Synna—"

The loud pop of gunfire cut off his next words, and the wood above my head splintered as a scream of pure terror launched from my throat.

Chapter 11

Tarek

Right Left Wrong (Three Days Grace)

My worst fear had come to pass.

The attacker was back, and this time he nearly killed us both. I had Synna on the ground so fast that I was afraid I hurt her, but she mumbled that she was alright.

"Don't move until I say. We're gonna crouch and then run to my truck. It's only a few feet away."

"Tarek," she whispered, the fear in her voice causing my coyote to hover near the surface. Shifters were protective by nature, but all bets were off when a mate was endangered. Our feral side took over.

My beast wanted to eliminate all threats and was ready to burst free. I couldn't let him take over, not yet, but I would as soon as Synna was safe. Since the attacker was on rez land, I could track him easier. His scent wouldn't be mixed in with the city and other humans, layers built upon layers of grime, sweat, and other odors.

"Now!" I whispered into her ear, giving her a slight boost before she ran for the far side of the truck, in the opposite direction of the shooter. I was right behind her and yanked on the handle, throwing open the door as she slid inside and sank to the floorboards. "Stay down!"

I scrambled across the seat, happy that I had emptied the truck's bed an hour earlier and had the keys in the ignition. My Ford was a '90s Ranger, but it hauled ass and was in good condition. We sped away from the hogan as my foot pushed the gas pedal to the floor. With every switch of the gears, I put more distance between us and danger.

"Call your brother. Tell Ronin we're leaving the rez and heading to the Rock."

I didn't hear Ronin's words clearly when he answered her call, but he was yelling as she filled him in, and I knew there'd be hell to pay for putting her life in jeopardy a second time.

None of us thought the attacker would be bold enough to come onto rez land. Not only that, but he shouldn't have known where I took Synna. Not many members of the Lords knew about my mother's hogan. I stayed in the clubhouse often. They knew I had a place but not the exact location.

There was only one explanation. Someone in the club had betrayed us.

The three-hour drive back to Flagstaff was full of tension. I was pissed and constantly gripped the steering wheel tight as thoughts of Synna hurt kept flashing through my brain.

My home was in Chinle and far from civilization. It was considered one of the safest cities in the entire U.S. Not to mention a spot that tourists enjoyed because of the beauty of the Canyons. The Grand Canyon was a scenic four-hour cruise from my hogan.

Fuck! How did this happen? Which one of my brothers was a rat?

The long drive from the rez was why I preferred to stay at the clubhouse.

The commute was too much to attempt on a regular basis. I usually stopped by the hogan a couple of times a month when life with the MC was slow. Hyde's Rock had plenty of room for the members, and it was easy to stay when I had my own bed to crash in and a door to lock behind me when I needed a little privacy.

"I'm not hurt, Tarek."

I shot a glance at her sideways, huffing under my breath. "Close enough."

"Try to calm down. I'm safe now. We're on our way to my brother. It's okay."

"No," I insisted. "It's not."

Synna was about to say something else when flashing lights caught my attention in the rearview mirror.

"Shit," I cursed. I was speeding. It didn't occur to me to watch the damn speedometer when I was trying to outrun a shooter who could have easily followed us. I'd planned to drive a slight detour and confuse anyone following our trail once we were closer to Flagstaff. Wasn't a point until we weren't surrounded by desert.

The clubhouse was still over an hour away.

I pulled over to the side of the road and yanked out my license and registration. The routine was nothing new. I tended to drive fast. These long, quiet roads were often empty, especially at night, and it didn't matter if I was in my truck or on my bike. I liked to feel the wind in my hair and freedom at my back.

The point was, I should have been more focused with Synna in the car.

There was a knock on my window, and I rolled it down, locking eyes with Sheriff Porter. Stifling a groan, I knew this was gonna be trouble.

"Speeding again, Jones?"

"It's an emergency."

He looked skeptical, lowering his head so he could see into the car. "You alright, Miss Daniels?"

Synna shook her head. "I don't feel well." She did look pale.

"I'm sorry to hear that. Do you need me to call a squad?"

Hell no.

"She'll be fine as soon as I get underway again."

He stroked his chin for a few seconds and then shook his head. "I need you to step out of the vehicle."

"Why?" I asked, narrowing my eyes.

"You've got several outstanding tickets. I'm going to have to bring you in."

What in the actual fuck?

There was absolutely no way I was leaving Synna alone right now.

The sheriff stood his ground. "Do I need to remind you that resisting arrest will violate your parole, Jones?"

Fuck. He was right. "Give me a second. I'm coming. I swear."

He nodded, watching my every move closely.

I turned to Synna. "I'm gonna open this door and step out. I want you to slide into the driver's seat and go straight to Ronin. Don't stop for any reason. Okay?"

Synna bit her lip, and I could tell she was afraid. "Okay."

"Hey," I called as she lifted her head. "I'm gonna be fine, and so are you." Brushing a quick kiss over her lips, I backed away. "Hyde and Ronin will know what to do."

I opened the door and stepped out as Synna slid into the driver's seat. "I'd like her to drive away now if it's alright. She's really not feeling well."

It was lucky that Sheriff Porter had known us both since we were kids. I had no idea why he was this far out on the highway, but luck wasn't on my side today.

He indicated that she could leave, and I watched her pull away from the curb. I didn't turn toward the sheriff until her taillights had disappeared.

"Let's go, Jones."

***

Synna

"YOU'RE GOING TO BE fine. So is Tarek," I reminded myself, talking aloud to relieve some of the anxiety and tension I felt. "You're almost at the Rock."

The drive seemed endless, and I was a mess by the time I arrived.

When I approached the main gate of the compound, I was forced to stop. Hyde had tightened security, and it was the worst time for that to happen. My gaze shifted to the rearview mirror as I watched for the shooter to jump out and fire at me again.

I didn't like being alone in the truck without Tarek. His absence caused my thoughts to run wild with speculation.

One of the prospects waltzed up to the door and peered inside, frowning.

"Where's Tarek?"

"Let me inside, dammit!" I screeched, and he hopped backward, running to do as I asked.

Nothing like a little female drama to light a fire under his ass.

I hit the gas pedal hard, and the engine seemed to lurch as I sped inside and parked close to the front entrance. My hands shook when I slid from the driver's seat as Hyde, Buzz, Ronin, and a few others ran toward the truck.

"Synna!" Ronin reached me first, his arms wrapping around my back as he hauled my body close.

"Tarek got arrested," I blurted, going off on a rant. "I'm scared half to death. Someone tried to kill me for the second time. There's a maniac on the loose. This isn't what I expected when I decided to come home early." Blinking back tears, I lifted my head from my brother's chest. "You need to get Tarek back for me. I swear I'm this close to losing it." I lifted my hand and spread two fingers an inch apart.

"Aw, Syn. I'm sorry. We will," he soothed. "I promise."

Buzz pulled me away from my brother, checking me over in a panic. "You're not hurt, right?"

"No, just shaken up," I admitted.

He hugged me, and then Hyde tugged me into his chest next. "Scared the shit out of me, Shortstack."

"For a bunch of tough bikers, you all hug a lot."

Hyde snorted as he released me. "Nothing happens to you, Synna. We're all pissed. This asshole is going down."

I knew that, and I loved them all for rushing to my side. "I think I could use a drink."

Buzz and Hyde chuckled as Ronin's arm draped around my shoulders, and he steered me inside. We walked straight to a booth in the corner of the bar, and he ordered water, beer, food, and a bottle of whiskey. The latter was for him. I sat back, chewing on my lip, watching Buzz and Hyde making phone calls.

"Tarek's gonna be fine. Always is. He's tough."

"Yeah, I know that."

"Do you?" Ronin sat back, clearly not believing me, as his arms crossed over his chest, and he scowled. "Something is different. I thought you hated Tarek."

"Then why did you leave me with him?"

"The rez is remote and safe. At least, it should have been. I thought it was the logical place to leave you until we sorted this mess. Although now I'm having doubts, especially with that look on your face."

"What look?" I asked with attitude.

"The one that tells me Tarek Jones messed with my sister."

I rolled my eyes at his words. "Oh, stop."

"He did, didn't he?" Ronin asked with a growl.

"Watch it, Ro. I'm not a child anymore."

"You're still under my protection. I already warned him once, not gonna—"

"What did you just say?" Instantly pissed, I wasn't the least bit sorry for cutting him off.

"I told him to leave you alone."

"When?" I asked, suddenly concerned that Ronin had done something awful. My stomach twisted at the thought.

"Four years ago, if you must know. I made it clear that he wasn't to touch you."

"Why?" I asked, tears filling my eyes. "How could you do that?"

"You were too young." He swallowed hard, refusing to meet my gaze as he looked down at the table. "I thought it was best to separate you."

Shocked and upset, I couldn't form any words for a full minute. "And Heather Downs?"

"He never touched her to my knowledge. She was just the means he used to push you away. I told him to figure it out because he wasn't messing up my sister's chance at a future. Heather was at the right place at the right time. It wasn't hard to convince you of his deceit. I don't believe they ever hooked up." Ronin sighed. "I'm sorry. Now that I'm saying all this, it does sound pretty shitty."

"I can't believe you intervened like that. Do you have any idea how much that tore me up? How badly that broke my heart?" I stood up, slamming my palms on the table. "You didn't have the right. I was eighteen. You ruined *everything*," I accused and slid from the table, running upstairs to one of the vacant rooms.

I was lucky when I found a couple that wasn't in use, and the keys were still in the locks. Visitors often took these rooms, especially brothers from other chapters.

Shoving into one and then slamming it shut, I snatched up the key, turned the lock, and then fell on the bed, releasing the tears that had been building since the moment I returned to Flagstaff.

Chapter 12

Synna

Blinding Lights (The Weeknd)

"Synna? We need to talk."

I'd spent the most awful, restless, lonely night of my existence. Every second that Tarek was gone, a terrible ache throbbed in my chest. It was silly to feel so strongly, but I reminded myself that I didn't just fall in love with him in the last few days. My heart was his four years ago. Time only prolonged the inevitable.

I missed Tarek so much that I hardly slept, and all I could think about was the couple of days of total serenity and euphoria we shared in his bed. That night in the rain would live in my memory for a long time. All I wanted was to feel his touch, become lost in his kisses and embrace.

Closing my eyes, I could almost sense his presence. The man had altogether ruined me for anyone else.

"Synna?" Ronin repeated, knocking on the door louder. "Please. It's important."

I rose to my feet and unlocked the door, sinking back onto the mattress as he walked inside, crossing my legs as I stared in his direction. "Well?"

My brother began to pace, cracking his neck and then his fingers. Ronin was agitated about something, and I had a feeling it wasn't what we discussed last night.

"There was a note this morning."

A note? "What kind of note?"

"A threat." He cleared his throat and finally met my gaze, his expression a mixture of concern, regret, and fear.

I wasn't used to seeing my brother afraid. Nothing ever scared him. "Ro?"

"The note was cryptic, but it named you specifically."

Frowning, I glanced down at his hand and noticed the blood on his knuckles. "What did you do to your hand?"

He blinked, somewhat dazed. "Smashed it, I think."

"Oh, Ronin." I stood up as he opened his arms in invitation, issuing a slight sniffle as I wrapped my arms around his thick waist. "Why did you hurt yourself?"

"Couldn't handle the thought of this killer finding and hurting you. I'm fuckin' livid, and I've never been so goddamn frightened in my life."

"Hey," I chided as I lifted my head. "Nothing is going to happen to me. I have you, Hyde, Buzz, and the whole club watching my back." Attempting to smile, I failed. "And I have my Tarek."

"Your Tarek?" he asked softly.

"Yes. I love him, Ronin. I did four years ago, and I do now."

He hung his head slightly. "I'm sorry I forced the two of you apart."

"I know."

I stepped out of his arms and led him into the bathroom.

"Sit on the toilet, dummy. I need to clean and bandage your hand."

Ronin stayed silent until I finished. "Hyde is on his way to pick up Tarek. I assume he'll want to see you right away."

"Did you speak to him?"

"No, but I will. I promise."

"Good. You owe him an apology." Tarek was never unfaithful, he didn't cheat on me, and he wasn't a liar. The only secrets he kept were the ones the MC obligated him never to speak. As a member of the Lords of Wrath, he swore an oath to his brothers. Tarek was loyal and always had been.

That wasn't why I was worried.

In the back of my mind was the thought that it didn't make sense. Why was I being targeted? Why would a random group of texts from Heather Downs show up on Tarek's phone the exact moment I walked back into his life?

"There's something else you should know. Tell Hyde right away, okay?"

He stiffened, standing up immediately. "What is it?"

"The day I arrived in Flagstaff, I stopped at the Bond office."

"Yeah, you told me."

"I forgot to mention that there was a note on my windshield after I left."

"What did it say?"

"Leave town or else."

Ronin sucked in a breath, a growl in his throat. "What did Tarek say?"

"I forgot to mention it to him, too," I admitted with a wince.

"Holy fuck, Syn. This is bad."

"I know," I agreed with a sigh. "I know. Okay?"

"He's gonna be even more pissed than I am."

"Yeah, you're probably right."

***

Tarek

THE JAIL CELL WAS empty as I entered, and I parked my ass on a metal bench as I tried not to worry about Synna. She should have arrived at the Rock by now. It had taken over an hour and a half to be processed and then placed in custody. I knew the routine. Unfortunately, this wasn't my first arrest.

I went down the wrong path for a bit after Synna left. I was lost without her, pissed off at the separation, and positive I would never get another chance to make things right. My coyote became almost feral.

As a result, I was reckless. I drank too much and started fights. Rode too fast on my Harley and took risks. Full of rage, I started fights so that I could brawl. Hell, I was taken aside and warned more times than I could count by both Buzz and Hyde.

When I didn't listen, Ronin and Hyde intervened and kicked my ass when they pulled me from the Rock, and I got wasted to the point that I hit one of my brothers.

Lost, I sped down the highway every chance I got and awaited fate to intervene. Nothing happened, and I knew it was my mother and the spirits of my people that protected and kept me safe.

Sheriff Porter got sick of seeing my face. I had a record by then and served a little time. I hated that asshole, but he helped set me straight, and I had to agree that I needed it. Those first two years Synna was gone were the longest.

Over the next two, I learned to deal with the separation, but I didn't realize how much I still wanted her until the day she came home, and I kissed her in that hidden alcove behind the bar.

Now, I craved her touch. Dreamed of her soft voice and silken hair, her sexy smile, and the seductive swing of her hips. Every part of Synna was tattooed on my heart like the tribal marks on my skin. She was permanently etched with black ink and wasn't going anywhere. I'd die to protect her, and there wasn't a single thing anyone could do to stop me.

"You've got a phone call."

Sheriff Porter was standing in front of the cell as I stood.

"Thanks."

He grunted in response.

Ronin was on the other line when I answered. "Hyde is on his way to bail you out, but we've got a big problem."

"What's that?"

"There was a note left outside the compound this morning. It was bloody and crumpled and attached to a dead lobo. Head was cut clean off with a sharp blade."

"What the fuck?"

"Yeah, that's not the worst part."

Shit. "Tell me."

"The note was a threat on Synna's life."

"What!?" I exploded, ignoring the dirty look Sheriff Porter shot my way at the outburst. "You better be right by her side."

"She's in the shower. You should know it's not the first note."

"She's had another?"

"The day she arrived. Syn said she forgot all about it, but it was on her windshield after leaving the Bond agency. Told her to leave town or else."

Dammit, Synna! She should have told me. "What else did the new note say?" There was more. Had to be. He sounded pissed but also apprehensive.

"Hyde thinks it's personal."

"Against Synna?"

"No. *You*," he emphasized. "The note read **An Eye for An Eye. You killed mine. I will kill yours**."

"No," I whispered. "Billy Forsythe?"

"That's Hyde's opinion."

"What about you?"

"Nothing else makes sense, Tarek."

"I agree." I had to do everything in my power to take out the Forsythe brothers as quickly as possible. It was the only choice. I hoped they would drop the ridiculous feud they had with our Bond agency and me, but that didn't appear to be the case. "I won't lose Synna."

"Then we both understand what's at stake."

"Yeah, we do."

Ronin hung up, and although it wouldn't be obvious to many when Ronin said those words, he meant that he would do everything and anything to keep Synna safe. Her life over mine if necessary. I couldn't fault him for saying so.

Billy Forsythe was Daniel Forsythe's brother. We'd had a bond for him over three years ago. It was supposed to be a routine pick up, just snatch the guy, and bring him in like usual. It didn't go down that way.

Daniel opened fire as we stepped onto his lot and hit Hyde in the leg. Ronin was shot in the shoulder. I was the only one who could defend us that day, and I shot back. The bullet hit Daniel in the chest, and he bled out before the ambulance arrived.

He was pronounced DOA.

Billy never forgave us for killing his brother, specifically me. He tried to have us all arrested, but it was self-defense, and he lost the case against our agency. The whole thing left bad blood between the numerous Forsythe brothers and cousins.

We lost half the bounty because Daniel wasn't brought in alive, and it hit the Bail Bond business hard for a few months.

Sheriff Porter never believed I wasn't somewhat responsible. He thought I could have taken Daniel down without gunfire. He just didn't get it.

The notes made sense now.

The Forsythe brothers were well known in Flagstaff. Two had gone to school with Synna. They knew I was dating her before she left for college. I wasn't sure how they knew she was coming home. That part was still a little sketchy, but I had no doubt Billy wanted revenge.

Unless someone in the club found out, that was the only way news of her arrival would have spread so quickly. Cracking my neck, I held back a growl as rage simmered under my skin.

This was the second time I felt the sting of betrayal. I kept it to myself until now since I didn't have enough information to take it to Hyde, but I wasn't staying silent anymore. Someone in the club was a narc. If it wasn't to the police, then they were feeding Intel to Billy Forsythe.

If I was right, that brother was going down hard.

Chapter 13

Tarek

Waking the Demon (Bullet for My Valentine)

"WE HAVE A RAT," I snarled, not waiting any longer to come to the point.

Hyde arrived thirty minutes ago and posted bail. Agitated by the delay in processing, I paced the length of the cell until I was freed.

He opened his mouth to reply but shut it when the sheriff strolled our way.

Sheriff Porter shot me an amused look as he took his time unlocking the door, giving me advice on being an upstanding citizen. In the past, I would have snickered in his face, but with Synna back in my life, I nodded, accepting his words with a tiny slice of humble pie.

Hyde noticed, smirking as he figured out what I was doing. Once we were out of earshot, he fixed me with one of his alpha stares.

"You're sure?" His hand rose, and he rubbed the back of his neck. "I have to take this seriously, and I don't like it, Tarek."

"That makes two of us." No one liked to think we had a rat or narc in the Lords of Wrath, but all the evidence pointed to the fact that someone had access to sensitive information and was sharing it outside of our club.

"Ronin said he keeps a tracker on Synna's cell. She doesn't know about it, but he put it there before she left for the university. Didn't want to take any chances. He was right to do it. We've got plenty of enemies."

True enough. "She'd be pissed if she knew."

"Oh yeah," he agreed.

"Tell me you're looking into this."

"I am. I already asked Ronin to be discrete. If someone has turned on the club, he'll find out."

I didn't doubt it.

We walked outside the precinct, and Hyde lit a cigarette, offering me a smoke. "You owe me now. Don't fuckin' blow off your court date."

"Yeah, yeah." I didn't care about that right now. I just needed to return to Synna.

"You don't need to worry. Synna is safe at the compound." He puffed away on his smoke, shaking his head as he watched me.

Ignoring his ass, I pulled out my phone and called her number. No answer. "She's not picking up." Without taking more than a couple of hits, I tossed the cigarette to the ground, stomping it out with my boot.

"Ronin said she was taking a shower and grabbing a bite to eat. It's a bit crowded at the Rock. Bandit and Ripper made it in a couple of days ago. Rael and Wraith came in yesterday afternoon. Don't worry. There's lots of protection."

"Right. I'm sure she'll call back soon."

Hyde and I quickly stopped for more smokes, a drive-thru for food since I was starving, and drove to the compound. The entire way, I felt off, like something just wasn't right. I couldn't shake the feeling and tried calling Synna again, but it went straight to voice mail. Taking a deep breath, I tried not to panic.

When Hyde pulled onto the lot and parked, I was out of the door before he shut off the engine. We usually liked to ride, but he opted for the cage since I didn't have my bike. I heard his chuckle and ignored it as I ran inside the Rock.

There were a few stragglers this early in the morning, but not many of my brothers were awake yet. I scanned the vicinity for Ronin and heard his booming voice coming from the common room. I had to wait to catch his attention since he was talking to Buzz.

"Bones wanted his ashes spread out across the ocean. Ain't that somethin'? Never liked the idea of being buried in the ground. Said his soul was meant to wander."

Ronin smiled sadly. "That was Bones for sure."

"I'm gonna ride through Nevada and check in with Crusher. Might even hit up the Royal Bastards and have a beer with Grim."

"Sounds like a plan."

"Would be fun for you to join me. I'd like some company when I toss Bones in."

Ronin laughed lightly. "I'm sure you'll have several brothers interested in coming with you."

"True. I'm looking forward to it. Gonna take off as soon as this mess is all settled. It's not right to keep Bones waiting."

"I agree."

Impatient, I left the room and decided to find Synna myself. After checking every room and waking up a few of my brothers who grumbled loudly at the intrusion, I didn't locate my mate. That feeling of uneasiness in my stomach intensified.

I walked back into the common room, my fists clenching as I approached a couple of my brothers from Nevada. Bandit and Ripper were playing pool against Rael and Wraith. Never seen a crazier lookin' bunch of bikers.

They were a welcome sight.

"I can't find Synna," I shouted, like that explained my nearly psychotic behavior.

Rael and Wraith had only met her once or twice, but Bandit and Ripper had partied with the Arizona Lords quite a bit. They knew Ronin's sibling well. She was like a little sister to nearly every member, including the Nevada chapter.

"What did Ronin say?"

"He's talking to Buzz. I didn't want to butt in."

Rael snickered as Wraith shook his head. "If it's important, better not wait long."

I ran a hand through my hair with mild agitation and stalked from the room, nearly bumping into Ronin.

"Have you seen Synna yet?" He looked as anxious as I felt.

"Nope," I answered. "Can't find her."

Ronin spun away from me and ran toward the stairs, bounding up two at a time to the second level. I heard his bellow of rage and knew my instincts were correct. Something was terribly wrong.

"Synna is missing."

I knew he would say the words before he did, but it still felt like a sucker punch to the gut. My palm landed against the nearest wall, and I fought the urge to shift into my coyote right there.

"Fight it," Hyde ordered as he walked in front of me, and I managed to gain control. "We can track her phone. Ronin, calm the fuck down."

"Fuck off, Hyde."

"That make you feel better, asshole?"

Ronin rolled his shoulders back, on the verge of losing his temper. "No."

"Man up. Rage doesn't help."

Ronin pulled out his cell, hit the app on his phone, and found Synna's location. I swear I didn't breathe until he answered. "She's not here."

"No shit," Hyde muttered.

I growled my response, unable to hold back. "Where?"

"On the road. My guess is the rez. She's headed that way."

"How far did she get?"

"She's got a forty-five-minute head start."

"Motherfucker!" I yelled, not bothering to listen to what anyone else had to say. My pres would get over it. Hyde knew how much I loved Synna. From the way he looked at me, I think he figured out that she was my mate.

I ran from the Rock, dropped onto the seat of my bike, and hauled ass from the parking lot. I could hear the sound of multiple Harleys joining my own, but I wasn't waiting for everyone to catch up. There was only one main road that she could have taken, and I planned to catch up to her fast. If I had any luck, I might prevent her from crossing onto rez land before she was hurt.

Gripping the handlebars of my bike, I focused on my breathing, trying to soothe the beast within. My mate was in danger. The coyote inside was unhinged. He would tear apart the entire desert to find her and then rip apart her attacker.

This enemy had awakened the demon within, the hunger to rend apart flesh as I destroyed the threat against my woman.

Billy Forsythe tried to take what was mine.

He was gonna be sorry he ever knew her name.

Chapter 14

Synna

Wolf Totem (The Hu)

Tarek WE NEED TO talk.

After missing him all night, it was strange that he didn't call. I expected to hear his voice as soon as he was out on bail, but all he sent was that text.

Me You okay? Missing you.

Tarek No. You should have told me about the note.

My heart sank. He was right, but I forgot all about it. Was he angry?

Me I'm sorry.

I didn't get a return text for several minutes and decided to try calling instead of texting. He didn't pick up. Was he so pissed he didn't want to speak to me?

Tarek Meet me at the hogan.

Tarek I'm almost there.

That was strange. With the shooter still on the loose, it seemed risky.

Me You sure it's safe?

Tarek Picked up the shooter. All good.

Relieved, I didn't question him about it further. His responses were cryptic, but I assumed he was frustrated, tired, and fed up. I couldn't blame him for feeling that way. I was sure I could smooth things over once I saw him.

Me I'll leave right now.

Tarek Good. Drive safe.

I still had Tarek's keys in my purse. I was about to tell Ronin where I was going when he sat down with Buzz. The two men fought their emotions as they talked about Bones. I didn't want to bother my brother and decided if Tarek said everything was safe, it didn't matter if I left without telling anyone.

This morning, the air was dusty and dry, and I picked up a bandana, tying it around my throat since I knew I would be back on the rez. The dust made my throat dry.

I was looking forward to staying in the hogan again. Funny, it didn't seem as primitive as when I first saw it. I started to think of it as a home during the time I stayed with Tarek. As long as he was with me, I'd be happy.

Halfway through my trip, I had to pull over. A haboob kicked up.

Dust storms were typical in Arizona with the dry desert landscape. If it wasn't the dense dust of a storm, then wildfires were usually causing a problem. Summer was so dry it was inevitable.

I gripped the steering wheel and waited impatiently for the weather to cooperate. Once it was safe, I was back on the road again.

I made excellent time despite the brief stop and parked Tarek's truck in the usual spot.

There was no sign of a storm here, and I shut the door with a loud click before I walked inside the hogan and looked for Tarek. I would have thought he would be there waiting, but there was no sign of him.

"Tarek?" I called out, shielding my eyes against the glare of the sun as I walked back outside.

No answer.

"Tarek!" I shouted, confused. Where was he?

Walking around the hogan and his property, I found no sign that he had been here at all. Swallowing hard, I walked back toward the truck. Was this a trick? Why would he do that?

This was ridiculous. I wasn't sticking around by myself out in the open.

A deep and disturbing growl from behind caused my entire body to stiffen. I turned around and lifted my hands, gasping at the enormous predator that stopped a short distance away, eyeing me like its next meal. The animal wasn't a wolf or mountain lion but appeared to be something that crossed over between the two. It was odd and disconcerting, frighteningly grotesque in a way that wasn't normal but something decidedly sinister.

Swallowing hard, I backed up a few paces.

The animal bared its teeth. Saliva dripped from the black gums as I tried not to panic.

I wasn't sure why my memory chose that moment to bring up the night the elder spoke of skin-walkers. It wasn't helpful, and I trembled in fear as the beast before me started to stalk slowly forward. The Navajo believed that skin-walkers were bad spirits and evil shifters. It wasn't hard to believe that concept as I stared into the ebony eyes of this monster.

I could swear that I saw intelligence in the eyes that shouldn't exist in an animal.

Was this some wanderer? A freakish experiment?

Or a real nightmare?

Pivoting on my left foot, I decided to run. It was foolish, but there weren't many options. I didn't think it through, just ran as fast as I could out into the desert. The canyons were close, and I didn't hesitate to try reaching higher ground.

The beast behind me nipped at my heels, and I screamed as I ran faster, nearly tripping in my haste. My feet stumbled, but I didn't falter, climbing the rocks and hoisting myself higher, hoping I could increase the distance between us.

I made it to the top of one of the smaller cliffs of the canyon and spun around, slowly backing away from the predator only a few feet away. It was toying with me. We both knew it.

I could have been ripped apart at any time.

The ledge was beneath my feet before I realized that I had backed up as far as I did. Glancing down, I knew I couldn't survive the fall. It was much too high. Severe injury or death awaited if I fell.

Moving my feet to the side, I slowly attempted to leave the cliff's edge.

The beast snarled, and I paused, taking one step back when the animal lunged. Screaming, I slipped and tumbled over the edge, crying out when I smacked into the hard rock and a little outcropping that just barely saved my life as I slammed into the jagged surface with my stomach. Sharp stabs of pain electrified my right side as I stifled a scream of agony.

My fingertips dug into a dip in the sandstone walls but barely held on. My body dangled above as my feet swung in the air. The creature lowered his head over the side, and I swear I saw the monster smile as his mouth opened and his teeth snapped.

When the elder told the story around the bonfire, he said a skin-walker must be called by its name, that it was a trickster that could take on other identities. I wished I knew this beast's name.

Sweat dripped into my eyes as my fingers began to slip. I thought I heard a scuffle and looked up at the exact moment that my fingers lost their grip.

A horrifying scream burst from my lips as a pair of strong arms reached out and caught my wrists.

Shocked, I gazed upward into Tarek's eyes. "I said I wasn't letting go, and I meant it."

"Tarek." Emotion churned so hard within that all I could do was tremble with the knowledge that I nearly fell to my death in the cavern below.

He hauled my body upward without much effort and hauled me into his embrace. His entire body shuddered. "I was almost too late."

"But you weren't."

He gave me a quick kiss and then spun, facing the beast that seemed to grow bigger than his size a few minutes ago. Confused, I could only watch as the two stared one another down. There was a strange sense of urgency and an electric charge that penetrated the air with expectancy.

In the distance, I thought I heard howling. This was the strangest experience I'd ever had.

It didn't end there.

Tarek's body began to change as he let loose an enormous growl. One second, he was the man I knew, and the next, he was a beast as big and intimidating as the one that chased me to this ridge.

My eyes widened, and I stumbled backward, falling flat on my ass.

Tarek just morphed into a wolf.

***

Tarek

My truck was already parked in front of the hogan when I arrived. I lifted my nose and caught a familiar scent that didn't belong to Synna, wondering why I had never picked up on it previously.

Maybe it was so close to home, so normal, that it never occurred to me that a friend would betray me. My suspicions that a brother had betrayed the club were confirmed. There was no time to dwell on it now.

None of that mattered since I needed to find Synna.

Hyde was right behind me, his tone angry when he realized the attacker's identity. "Go! She's in danger!"

I heard Synna's scream and never ran so fast in my entire life. The world tilted on its axis, and my heart nearly burst right through my chest when I followed the trail, snarling when I saw her hovering on the canyon ledge, her fingers slipping as she desperately tried to hang on. The shifter hovering close by was methodically hunting her, forcing her closer to the edge so she would fall.

I was never going to make it in time.

My coyote howled as I saw her tumble backward, and I lunged for the edge, barely catching her in time. My hands shot out as I threw myself to the ground. I was breathing so hard I thought I might pass out.

My only thought was to return her to safety, tugging her upward and away from the dangerous canyon below. Once I had her in my arms, I kissed her quickly and gently pushed her behind me.

My coyote would no longer be contained. Our mate needed us.

Like most predators, hunger or rage were usually the catalysts for a shift. Strong emotions were hard to hold back and rein in. Shapeshifters were much more powerful than average humans. It wasn't hard to figure that out, but most people didn't believe it, even when they saw it with their own eyes.

We were extremely fast, agile, impossible to catch, and more intelligent than the average beast.

I knew Synna would be shocked when she saw my transformation, but there was no holding the coyote back. I wondered briefly if she believed the legends that the elders told around the bonfire.

Would she consider me a threat? Evil? There was no way of knowing.

I didn't bother looking in her direction as I focused on my enemy and the brother who betrayed his club. None of us could have known he was hacking into the phones and devices of the members and using them for Intel. He told secrets to the Forsythe brothers, Sheriff Porter, and who knew how many others. Once Ronin went digging, he found plenty of incriminating evidence. The last few hours had been enlightening.

The only thing that baffled me was his target.

Synna never did a thing to Whiskey Sue's son J.D.

I charged into the betrayer's side and knocked him to the ground before he rose with a roar. Sharp claws slashed at my flank and missed. I bared my teeth and snapped at his shoulder, ripping into the flesh. If I had to, I would take him out a piece at a time.

He shook my jaw free, and we circled one another, prepared to go in for the kill.

"Synna!"

Ronin's voice was off, but I didn't notice that he had shifted until I saw the impressive broad wingspan of his eagle. Synna gasped as he swooped in and struck J.D. in the eye. His wolf let out an odd noise somewhere between a screech and a yelp of pain, using his giant paw to cover the wound. The eagle soared high and returned for another strike when J.D. suddenly turned his focus on my mate. He lumbered toward Synna, and I leaped into the air, landing on his back. My jaws opened wide, and I gripped his neck, careful not to snap it as I slammed his body down on the rock.

He wasn't dying. Not yet.

J.D. needed to answer to the club.

His death wasn't my kill alone.

Chapter 15

Tarek

All Animal (Through Fire)

"A<small>RE YOU SURE YOU'RE</small> alright?" I asked for the tenth time, holding Synna on my lap as I perched on the tailgate of my truck. This was a lot to take in. She must have been completely overwhelmed, not to mention confused and scared. Her reality had changed, and both her brother and her mate were at the center of it.

"I'm fine," she insisted as her brow furrowed. "What are you again?"

"A shapeshifter."

"And Ronin?"

"The same."

"But not evil, right? I don't sense any evil with either of you."

"Well, no. The whole club is shifters, honey. None of us are evil." Unless you counted J.D.

"Why did J.D. look so odd compared to the two of you? Is he one of those skin-walkers?"

"No, but I can see why you would think that. I don't know why he's different. Obviously, he was dabbling in things we didn't know about."

"I see." She had a glazed look in her eyes, and I knew she would need time to come to terms with all of this.

"It's gonna be okay, I promise," I assured her.

"I know." Her gaze met mine as she tilted her head to the side. "I think I'm a little shocked."

"Yeah," I agreed, "but you'll accept it once your brain has a chance to think it over."

"I hope so."

"You know the great thing about us? Shifters have incredible senses. That's why we're such great bounty hunters and trackers. We have a reputation for not losing our bond."

She smiled a little with my words.

"We can track anyone, anywhere, and that's even more important when it comes to our mate."

"Mate?"

"Yeah, the one we love and bond with. The female that is our one true love. There's no place you could go that I couldn't find you. No matter what the future holds, know that I will always come after you. You're mine, Synna Daniels." Our lips met as I leaned in and captured a kiss. "But I'm yours too."

"I guess the two of you are together now, huh?" Ronin stood awkwardly, shuffling from foot to foot. He cleared his throat loudly. "I owe you an apology, Tarek."

"For?" I asked, wrapping my arm around Synna.

"Separating you from my sister. I won't intervene again."

"Good."

"Unless you hurt her, cheat, or piss her off. Then I can't guarantee a thing."

Chuckling, I nodded. "I suppose I'll deserve it then."

Synna stood up and walked into Ronin's arms as he opened them. "Thank you."

"Anything for you, Syn."

"Since you're a shifter too, what does that mean for me?" She gazed upward and into his startled eyes.

"I've never seen any indication that you have the ability. I wasn't sure for a long time, but you've never shifted or struggled with the same emotions and urges. I think it must have skipped over you somehow."

"How is it possible that you can change into an eagle?"

"Our father was a shapeshifter. He told me when I was young. I was about six when I first showed signs. He asked me to keep an eye on you, and I always have."

"You did," she agreed. "You're pretty awesome," Synna admitted, lifting on her tiptoes to kiss his cheek. "But stay out of my business from now on." I could tell she was only half-joking. "And no more secrets. Okay?"

Ronin laughed as he squeezed her tighter. "I promise to try."

He released her, and she sat back down on my right as her fingers slipped into mine. "I owe you an apology too. I should have said something about that first note. It might have made a difference."

"I'm not angry. I don't know that it would have mattered. J.D. was looking to start trouble, and it was only a matter of time before he stirred up enough shit to cause problems."

"True enough." She sighed softly. "At least I know that you've always been faithful. You didn't lie, and you didn't cheat. I was pissed when Ronin admitted he separated us on purpose, but now that we're together, I just want to move forward and forget that part of our past."

"Me too," I whispered, tugging her closer as I placed a kiss on top of her head.

Hyde approached as he ticked his chin in my direction. "It's time."

"I'll be back soon." I squeezed Synna's hand and then slid from the tailgate of my truck.

"I know. Be safe." Synna pressed her lips to mine, and I nearly forgot what I needed to do. "I'll be waiting for you inside the hogan."

Now that was enough reason to move club business along.

With a wicked grin, I winked in her direction and then joined my brothers.

***

J.D. WAS STRAPPED DOWN to a chair when I entered the oversized shed on my property. He'd been beaten in my absence, and I wasn't the least bit sorry that he was already paying for his betrayal.

"You're just in time," Hyde announced as he held up a blowtorch. "Things are about to get a little heated."

Smirking, I gave him a nod of agreement.

J.D. struggled, spouting off threats and profanity. None of his words fazed any of us. And no amount of movement loosened the bonds we used to hold him down. Even if he tried to shift, we'd be on him so fast his ass would never even make it up from the seat.

"I'd like to know why you targeted Synna. It still doesn't make sense to me."

I walked up close and folded my arms across my chest.

"We know you hacked into personal cell phones. There was a ton of computer equipment and devices in your room. You sent those notes just to spook Synna and start shit with me. Why?"

J.D. tilted his head back and laughed. "None of you figured it out, did you?"

"Figured out what?" Buzz asked, clearly agitated.

I was sure it stung badly that the son of his one true love was a backstabbing piece of shit. There would be lots of Johnny Cash playing in the near future.

"Billy Forsythe is my cousin."

Shocked, I turned to Buzz, who appeared even more surprised than I was. "Impossible."

"Is it? My mother left your ass because she couldn't bear the truth. She didn't want you to think less of her when I threatened to expose her past."

Buzz let out a growl that shook the walls so hard a few tools hit the ground. "You'll pay for your betrayal, J.D. Mark my words."

J.D. didn't seem to care, unfazed.

"Your punishment is twofold. Your patch will be burned from your back, and then you'll be released for the hunt. The Lords of Wrath will serve pack justice. Better make your peace with God, boy. You won't survive the night."

J.D. began yelling again, but no one else said a word as Hyde turned on the blowtorch and slowly began to burn off the tattoo that once made him a brother in our MC. Somewhere during the process, J.D. passed out. I picked up a bucket and filled it from the well, dumping it over his head.

Dazed, he fought against his restraints as we were called every name he could think of, every insult he could conjure. Didn't change a damn thing.

Untying the rope that held him in place, Buzz let J.D. stumble from his chair as he collapsed on the floor. He slowly stood to his feet and flipped us all off before running out and into the desert. We'd find him. After all, we had help.

"Time for the hunt, boys," Hyde announced.

One by one, we all began to shift. Bears, coyotes, wolves, eagles, mountain lions, and even a jaguar let loose as the club sprang forward to track J.D. down.

Rael and Wraith let out their Reapers, their faces morphing into ghostly specters that caused the hair on my body to stiffen as my coyote lowered his head, conceding to the dominant, more ruthless beast in the room.

"Don't worry," Rael assured me. "We aren't capturing your prey's soul."

Holy shit! These Royal Bastards weren't guys I wanted as an enemy.

I led the way as I shifted, my paws pounding into the rock and desert sand. Justice would be served this night, swift and without mercy.

This was one hell of a day to remember.

J.D. would never harm anyone again.

***

Synna was waiting for me inside the hogan just as she promised. Already naked on the bed, she was so enticing that I growled as I stripped and quickly joined her. Not a moment to waste, I climbed on the bed and over her supple body, my thick cock swollen with the need to possess her again.

Her eyes dipped downward, and she licked her lips, noting that I wasn't in the mood to take this slow. "I need you."

I didn't hesitate to part her thighs as lust and desire dominated my brain. It wasn't going to be fast and hard, but I wanted to skip all the foreplay. There was plenty of time for exploration later.

My coyote was prodding me to make her mine. I slid a finger through her slick folds and then shuddered as I found her wet and ready.

"Been playing while I was gone?"

"Maybe," she teased.

"That's sexy as hell."

Fisting my dick, I pumped a few times, groaning as I watched her reaction, grunting when I saw the need in her eyes. No more wasted time. Not even a second between us. I positioned the crown of my cock at the entrance of her eager sex and slowly pushed the tip inside her. "I need to claim you," I whispered.

"Haven't you done that already?"

I shook my head. "No. I have to bite you. It won't hurt, not much."

"Take me, possess me, claim me, Tarek," she breathed out huskily. "That's all I want."

I began to slide into her as she moaned, and her legs fell open wider. Her tight pussy seemed to suck me in, and I groaned, thrusting the rest of the way as I buried myself fully to the root.

Chest to chest, we were as close as we could get.

"*Shijéí Naa Nish'aah*," I whispered in her ear, gliding slowly in and out as my hands rose and grasped her own above her head. My hips pumped with just enough motion that I could feel every part of her slick walls gripping my dick and pulling me deeper. Holding back a hiss of pleasure, I translated for her in English. "I give you my heart. Today. Tomorrow. Forever."

"Forever," she agreed as my mouth met hers, tangling our tongues in a delicious dance.

As my pace increased and her legs began to quiver, I knew she was close. My mouth separated from her lips and pressed kisses to her skin, trailing down the column of her throat to that spot close to her shoulder.

No longer holding back, my canines lengthened, and I bit down hard, sinking my teeth into her flesh. The metallic tang of her blood coated my tongue as she writhed beneath me, bucking her hips as she shuddered. Her walls clamped down on my cock as I lifted my head, sealing the wound with my saliva before pounding into her harder, so turned on that I forgot everything but being buried in my mate.

"Tarek!"

"I love you," I panted, plunging into her a few more strokes before my body tingled and I came, flooding her channel. "My beautiful mate."

Staring into her eyes, I knew the vision I had seen was true.

Synna was mine, and I was hers. Always.

Epilogue

Hyde

THIS HAD BEEN THE longest and most exhausting week in memory. All of the mess with J.D. had caused a shitstorm. It was evident that our enemies were closing in, and I didn't doubt the Forsythe clan was gonna cause more problems in the future. The fact that J.D. fed Intel to numerous other individuals was a notable cause for concern. I knew he involved Heather Downs and Sheriff Porter. Time would reveal who else was coming after the club.

I was on my way out of the office late Friday afternoon when I heard the bell ding above the front door. It wasn't a usual time for customers, but I picked up my satchel and slipped my cell phone into the inside pocket of my cut. I usually skipped wearing it during the day when I was behind the desk pushing paperwork, but it was closing time, and I had shit to do.

My jaw nearly hit the floor when I rounded the corner and spotted the gorgeous girl standing just inside the entrance. I'd never seen her around town before. If I had, I'd remember those luscious curves and that long hair that brushed her waistline.

"How can I help you?"

"I'm looking for someone." She seemed a bit nervous. "Tarek Jones. Is he working?"

I wasn't about to give out personal info on a brother to a stranger, no matter how smokin' hot she was. "Why are you looking for Tarek?"

My reaction must have been obvious. "Hey, I'm not looking for trouble. This is important."

Folding my arms across my chest, I wasn't giving her any information about the MC unless she had a good reason. "Tell me."

"I'm Tribal's daughter."

My jaw dropped, and I realized that I could see the resemblance for the first time. Thick, straight black hair, high cheekbones, almond-shaped eyes with a golden sparkle, strong bone structure. Hell, this girl only looked a couple of years younger than Tarek. His dad skipped town before his mother even knew she was pregnant. This young woman might have been telling the truth.

My arms dropped. "Well, you got a name, Tarek's sister?"

"Kaylani Jones."

I couldn't resist letting my gaze linger over her curves, settling for just a moment on the inward dip of her waist and then following the flair of her hips down those toned and sexy thighs. The kind of thick and muscular girl that was slender but athletic. Visions of those same thighs wrapped around my waist pounded in my head in time with my pulse.

The bear within snarled and rushed to the surface, and I held back a growl that confirmed why I reacted so strongly. Her scent drifted along like a perfume concocted to lure me in, tantalizing and sweet as raw honey. My cock stiffened as I imagined how pure and perfect she would taste.

My bear wanted Kaylani Jones. Scratch that. He needed to claim her.

Fuck me.

This girl was gonna be trouble.

No doubt about it.

Thank you for reading!

The series will continue with *Hyde*, Lords of Wrath MC #2.

If you enjoy MC romance and shifters, check out these books from the author:

Mystic Hallows Harem

Fallen from Grace

Crow

Haunted Wolf

Onyx

Harleigh

Feral Breed

Dark Promise

Carnage

The Biker's Gift

ARIZONA

Pres – Hyde (black bear)

V.P. – Ronin (bald eagle)

SGT at Arms – Digger (gray wolf/lobo)

Enforcer – Tarek (coyote) Navajo

Secretary – Bomber (gray wolf/lobo)

Treasurer – Cale (mountain lion) Apache

Road Captain – Phantom (hawk)

Member – Quill (mountain lion)

Member – Saber (jaguar)

Buzz (Retired Pres, black bear)

NEVADA

Pres – Crusher (gray wolf)

V.P. – Smokey (black bear)

SGT at Arms – Claw (mountain lion)

Enforcer – Bandit (coyote)

Secretary – Ripper (gray wolf)

Treasurer – Fury (fox)

Road Captain – Vapor (Hawk)

Navajo Translation

Yá' át' ééh (hello)
Nizhóní (beautiful)
Ayóó Áníínishní (I love you)
Yee naaldlooshii (skin-walker)
Nídin séli̱´i̱´ shijéí bináká hoodzą́ (missing you left a hole in my heart)
Shijéí T'áá Hazhó'ó Niba' Iiłkił (my heart slowly ticks for you)
Shijéí Naa Nish'aah (I give you my heart)

If you'd like to learn more about the Dine' culture or Navajo Nation, you can browse the websites below.

https://www.navajo-nsn.gov/history.htm
https://www.discovernavajo.com/navajo-culture-and-history.aspx
https://www.britannica.com/topic/Navajo-people
https://www.legendsofamerica.com/navajo-skinwalkers/

Sneak Peek

Ridin' for Hell, Royal Bastards MC

"Y<small>OU DON'T WANT TO</small> do this, *bruh.*"

This piece of shit really had no idea how much I actually *did* want to do this. I fuckin' lived for it. Breathed it. Inhaled violence, blood, and death in like oxygen just to make it from one minute to the next. I couldn't function, couldn't survive through the day without my sinister addiction.

My need to rip things apart and destroy flesh was a basic and integral part of the gruesome monster I had become. Nothing else was nearly as important as the vengeance that focused every fuckin' decision I made.

Shit. I was created to fuck people up.

And I got off on it like a *goddamn* drug.

"My pres is gonna have your ass, motherfucker," my prisoner yelled, spittle flying from his busted mouth. The drool was a mixture of blood and saliva as it dribbled down his chin. My gaze followed the movement of the fluid, almost gleeful at the fact that I was inflicting harm.

"Oh?" I asked calmly, unrolling my bag of delightfully sharp steel toys. "I'll remember that." Pausing to scratch my jaw, I shrugged as he narrowed his eyes. "I don't take it up the ass, boy. Maybe you do? Or your pres?"

"Fuck you!" he shouted, wiggling his body, and only succeeding in tightening the bonds wrapped around his thick, meaty wrists. The fucker really needed to lose a few pounds. His chubby gut wobbled every time he jiggled.

"I'm not into men although I do have a club member who is." Turning to Mammoth, I ticked my head in his direction. "Wanna a treat while I get everything ready?"

Mammoth chuckled, folding his arms across his massive chest as he silently appraised the punk dangling like a hunk of raw beef and stripped down to nothing but a pair of boxers. A meat hook secured to the main support beam above held him firmly in place, his feet scraping along the ground with every movement, not quite low enough to stand and much too high to rest on his knees. It was uncomfortable on purpose.

"I'd tear him apart," Mammoth answered with glee. "He'd be shitting blood for a month."

Mammoth wasn't gay but at six-foot-seven he was big as a fuckin' beast and rumor had it that he was packin' some serious meat down below. Of course, that was conjecture spread among the little club girls who kept us all company. But the Scorpions MC member who was cussing us out earlier had paled with Mammoth's words and didn't know any of that shit.

Mammoth never changed his expression, just kept those dark blue eyes focused on our prey.

"Let me go!"

A bold and pointless demand. He wasn't leaving this room. At least, not alive.

I was kind of hoping he'd piss himself soon with fear, especially once he realized he'd awakened to his last hours on this earth when the asshole climbed out of bed this morning.

Mammoth's lips twitched when our eyes briefly met, and I knew he was waiting for the same thing.

We were sick fucks, no doubt about it.

"How many years did you serve in Ely again?" Ely State was a fierce maximum-security prison in our home state of Nevada. Hell, the state's only death row inmates were housed there. It was no joke.

Mammoth smirked. "Five."

The Scorpion prisoner went completely still as he listened to our words.

"I can't remember what the conviction was," I replied casually, running my finger over the edge of a large hunting knife. "Murder?"

"That's what the judge said," Mammoth confirmed, his gaze never wavering from our prey. "Among others."

"They ever find the fucker you were convicted of killing?"

"Nah," Mammoth replied with a wide grin. "Too many pieces. Scattered them all over the state."

That was when our guest decided to start shouting as loud as he could. Gave me a fuckin' headache. "Grab him," I snarled as I walked over to a flat, stainless-steel table that we used for interrogations.

A high, load-bearing ability with a maximum weight capacity of 1,000 lbs. and guaranteed not to break. Or so the manufacturer boasted. It was for made for hunters with bulky, heavy prey like elk or human cadavers that were morbidly obese. I liked the idea of the second option.

Glancing at Mammoth, I was reminded why we needed such an expensive table in the first place. He was over three hundred pounds of solid muscle alone and when he was holding someone down it was imperative the damn piece of equipment didn't snap beneath the strain. That happened once. Wasn't pretty. Took forever to clean up the bloody mess.

Chuckling lightly, I picked up a long steel rod used for sharpening knives and a hammer. Walking over to the Bloody Scorpions MC member, I lifted the objects before his eyes. "I think you need a little motivation. We've been enjoying each other's company for over an hour now. I'm getting hungry and soon I'm not going to have any patience left."

Mammoth was busy strapping the guy down and securing him so that he wouldn't be able to move while I did my thing. Picking up the guy's right hand, I pressed it flat against the table as Mammoth held his wrist in place.

"I'm gonna fuck you up!"

"What's your name?" Mammoth asked, staring down at our prey as he struggled. "I wanna know whose mama I'm fuckin' tonight after I gut you like a squirming little fish."

"Fuck you!" He spit in Mammoth's face and missed as one of Mammoth's fists closed around his throat.

"Do it, Rael." My V.P.'s voice was calm, deadly quiet in a way that almost frightened *me*, and I was one of his best friends. "I ain't squeezin' yet."

Shit. Mammoth was pissed.

Maybe I should have asked one of my Enforcers like Exorcist or Jigsaw instead of Mammoth. His short fuse was gonna explode any second now.

Better speed things up.

I settled the metal rod over the center of the guy's hand, picked up the hammer . . . and slammed it down as hard as I could. A bloodcurdling scream launched from our prey's mouth as the rod punctured the table and pierced his flesh. The rod was shoved directly through the center of his hand and wobbled above like a floppy dildo.

Chuckling, I couldn't help but stare at the blood that leaked from the wound and dripped onto the concrete floor, trickling closer to the drain I had installed years ago in the center of the room.

I was kind of pissed that I didn't watch my strength and drilled a hole through the table, but my Reaper didn't hold back, especially when I was occupied with my number one obsession.

Revenge.

"Your name?" I asked, walking around the table and over to my workbench.

All the guy did was yell and cuss, his body flailing until Mammoth began to squeeze. "Last chance," he muttered. "I'd answer if I were you."

Choking and sputtering, the BSMC member tried to speak. Mammoth loosened his grip.

"Tiger."

"Your real name, not the pussy ass excuse for a road name," Mammoth demanded, shaking his head in annoyance.

"Biff Declan."

I snorted as Mammoth chuckled. "Your mama not like you any, boy?"

Biff cussed under his breath. "Fuck off."

Shaking my head, I ignored the agitation that surfaced. I needed answers, not to lose my shit or let Mammoth take Biff's life before I was ready. Sighing, I picked up a mallet and swung it around in the air.

"Your knees are next."

The door opened across the room and Exorcist walked in, his bloodshot blue eyes assessing the situation quickly before he snorted in humor. "Thought I'd pop in and check on my two favorite brothers."

Mammoth smirked. "Right. You'll get your turn. I want my piece first."

"What did he do to you?" Ex strode our way, all swagger as he lit up a cigarette.

"Spit in his face," I answered, trying not to laugh at Mammoth's expression of fury at the reminder. "But this asshole is mine until I say I'm done."

Ex nodded, immediately understanding this was personal. I didn't have to go into detail. The whole club knew my past. It wasn't a secret.

"My pres is gonna kill every last one of you Bastards!"

Biff must be feeling brave again. *Dumb fucker.*

Taunting my Reaper was a bad idea. That motherfucker had a bad temper and a short fuse, and he *always* came out to play. There was a reason I was the club Sgt. at Arms. I handled the hard shit. The jobs no one else wanted to deal with because it was messy. Thing was, I loved to lose control. When I was angry, my Reaper couldn't be held back. And then the *real* fun began . . . only to cause a shitstorm of carnage and destruction that dripped crimson and left everything in ruin.

Sort of like my past.

Sure, I'd been promoted to SAA, but I started out an Enforcer and that shit was in my blood. I didn't get to play as much as I liked anymore and that had a hell of a lot to do with my personal vendetta. I was only participating in this particular interrogation because this asshole worked for the same guys I was after. The ones who took *everything* from me.

Rage bubbled under the surface of my skin and I felt my Reaper stir. "How's Razr handling his new position? Missing Acid any?"

Biff was still for a moment and then started fighting against his bonds again, only succeeding in wearing himself out as he screamed threats and profanity.

"Yeah, yeah," I mumbled, twirling the mallet in my hand again. "Answer my questions."

Biff glanced at his hand and the rod still anchoring his palm to the table's surface. He paled a little more. "He's pissed. Your club is going down."

"Razr picked the wrong club to fuck with this time," Exorcist interjected.

"Who's supplying his whores?" I asked, moving closer and lifting the mallet. "Give me a name."

"Fuck you!"

Whack. The mallet hit his right knee as I swung, and a loud crack could be heard as the bone shattered. Biff's screams echoed in the room as I walked around the table, leaning down. "The left knee is next."

His words were almost slurred from the guttural screams that left his throat and the hoarse tone of his voice. "The Russian."

I already knew that. Needed more detail. "*Which* Russian?"

Cursing, Biff shook his head. "Vlad."

Vladimir Solonik. Russian *Bratva* or mafia. *Fuck.*

"When's the last time he visited your pres?"

Biff's eyes were glazed over with pain. He needed to answer before he passed out.

"When?" I demanded.

"They'll kill me," he finally answered, head turning to the side as his eyes fluttered.

Exorcist tossed his cigarette down and smashed it with his boot before turning on the sink. He filled a bucket half full and walked over to the table, dumping it over Biff's head. Sputtering and cursing, Biff yelled for several minutes.

"When?" I asked again, swinging the mallet close to his left knee.

"Please," Biff begged. "Fuck! Please stop."

His pleas fell on deaf ears. Neither Mammoth, Ex, nor I gave a shit. It was far too late to bargain.

"Answer," Mammoth snarled, his patience gone.

"Last Friday night," Biff whispered as our eyes met.

"You know anything else?"

"No," he replied firmly. "Razr didn't call church. He met with the Russian alone."

I believed the guy. My Reaper could sense when someone was lying. Biff was more afraid of the Russians than us. *Stupid.* He would die at our hands as soon as Mammoth and Exorcist were done with him. Suddenly fatigued, I dropped the mallet on my workbench. This shit didn't matter as much as finding that Russian fucker Solonik.

"Go, Rael. We're gonna finish this." Mammoth knew what I needed. Didn't have to say a word.

My gaze met Ex's and he ticked his head toward the door, a cruel smile twisting his lips. "We're gonna have some fun."

I didn't hesitate to leave the room, my thoughts a chaotic mess. Biff's screams echoed in the hall as I trudged upstairs. Most of the brothers and *cookies* were already busy in their rooms. A few were passed out on the leather couches spread around the perimeter.

No one was behind the bar. I poured a shot of Jack and tossed it back, letting the burn tickle my throat. After another, I set the bottle down and exited the clubhouse. Shadow, Toad, and another new prospect were posted at their usual positions.

I needed a ride and a smoke.

Even though that interrogation was over, I still felt restless, like my skin was crawling with unruly veins beneath the taut layers and an itch I couldn't quite scratch tormented my every waking moment. The need to claw at the walls of my body until they were neat, slithering little ribbons of perfectly torn flesh pulsed underneath my skin. It wasn't the first time I had daydreams or visions of blood, horror, or carnage.

The Reaper was a crude and vicious bastard. He always received what he wanted.

In this life, you reap what you sow.

A lesson I learned all too well.

Time was a brutal teacher as much as experience. Blind vengeance had ruled my actions and decisions for so long I wasn't sure how much was my own desires or how much belonged to the Reaper. We were too integrated now. Too woven together to know where I ended, and he began. It was what it was.

A choice made out of desperation. Binding for eternity.

Not everyone wanted to run from their past. Some souls embraced the chance to hunt their prey and seek vengeance. To inflict suffering and bring death, and to wield the power of the Reaper until vengeance had been served. I was one of the ruthless Bastards that liked the carnage just a little too much. Victory drew closer with every breath I took.

But the past never left me, never completely diminished, and constantly haunted my dreams as much as my reality. Every minute of the day brought my vengeance closer to completion. A bitter and resolute countdown that began six years ago. The day I lost it all. And it wasn't just me. My best friend Jameson's suffering was as great as my own . . .

It was time to exact justice. I was going to find that Russian fucker Solonik. And my Reaper would make him pay.

Ridin' for Hell, Royal Bastards MC is available now!

Sneak Peek

Sins of the Father, Ravage Riders MC

"I HEARD YOU WERE looking for answers again, Edge."

His sneer was unmistakable, along with the hatred and loathing in his voice. There was no love lost between us. Our arrangement was born of necessity, not respect. *Keep your friends close and your enemies closer.*

I smiled lazily, ignoring the urge to cough or choke. Without warning, I leaned forward and headbutted him as hard as possible, right on the nose. He dropped his hands from my shirt but pummeled my gut a few times as we staggered. I blocked one of the hits and swung my fist in a perfectly timed left hook.

Old southpaw.

I'd trained hard to be able to hit like that, with just enough accuracy, speed, and strength to take someone down but not inflict permanent damage. Rafe was a fool to try to take me on now. I'd trained faster and harder than most guys in the MC, and I seemed a natural at boxing. Now that I thought about it, I wasn't the only one. Most of my MC brothers were decent boxers. We could brawl with the best and take hits that would knock most guys out cold. And we were strong, resilient, tough fighters.

All except Rafe. Maybe if he stayed sober long enough, he could train and clean his act up, but I doubted it. *Lazy son of a bitch.* I pulled my punch a little, bored already. I wanted to see this asshole get what he deserved, but it wasn't the right time.

For now, I had to protect myself and any connection to the woman I loved. *Someday soon, asshole.*

Rafe laughed and wiped his nose on the sleeve of his shirt, blood dripping down the front as he sniffed. "You're getting better, quicker. Good for you, Edge."

I didn't acknowledge his words but kept my fight stance, ready for more. *Don't ever let your guard down.* I learned that shit the hard way. Those first few years were brutal teachers. The scars on my body proved my endurance and stamina and my ability to adapt to the harsh, vicious environment I was thrust in.

"No more tonight. You did good, kid. Get some pussy and celebrate. We'll pick this up tomorrow."

I didn't doubt our conversation would involve some serious shit later. Rafe didn't like it when I tried to dig into the MC's past and the connection to the Outlaws. *Too bad.* He didn't have a choice because I would do whatever the fuck I wanted anyway. As he walked away, I shook my head. The RRMC needed new leadership.

"Bro, where you been?"

R.J. clapped his hand on my shoulder, and I forced a smile, breathing slowly through my nose until I was calm. "Had a little talk with Rafe."

He frowned but didn't ask what it was about. *Good.* I hated explanations.

"Let's get out of here. Ghost wants to see if he can get lucky at the bar. Valan and Jake are antsy. They think G.Q. will snag all the ladies."

I snorted with humor. "He probably will. Pretty fucker."

R.J. laughed as he pulled me from the clubhouse, swinging his fist into my side, and we wrestled like we did when we were kids, knocking each other into walls on the way out. Out of breath and grinning like fools, both of us straddled our hogs. Seconds later, the loud heavy roar of our bikes filled the air as we headed to our favorite bar Crazy Eights.

You'd think it was a hardcore biker bar, but it wasn't. That was why we liked it.

The front doors were made of heavy wood and scraped the rough, uneven floor when you entered. Loud music and the familiar buzz of dozens of voices greeted you instantly as well as the smell, like a mixture of licorice and fried food. The main focal point was a large rectangular carved bar wrapped around the room and shaped like the number eight. Bartenders stood in the two circles, passing out drinks and taking orders.

A large kitchen sat at the northern end, serving appetizer-type foods like fries and chicken wings. Eight pool tables were scattered around the outskirts of the room while wooden tables and chairs hovered in the center. Everything was in multiples of eight. Interesting concept.

No live band played tonight, but the jukebox loudly blared out tunes. A modest-sized stage was set up on the far end. Entertainment was usually only Thursday through Saturday nights. A dance area, nothing more than a tiled square floor occupied the space in front of the stage, and off to the right was equipment set up for a D.J. Strobe lights dangled from above the dance floor, where it would light up as the gyrating bodies pressed close together to the beat of the music.

I could see how this place appealed to both the average and biker crowd. People were milling about all over the room, shooting pool, drinking beers, smoking cigarettes, and hanging around the jukebox making selections.

I ushered my guys toward the only open pool table that had suddenly cleared for our use. We never had to ask. A pool table would always open up when we walked in the door. Yeah, it was part of the biker persona and the culture of fear that kept the locals at a distance, but I didn't give a fuck.

We weren't here to make trouble. The owner was a brother, and we promised not to start shit in his bar. I picked up the chalk and decided to break, taking the first game with R.J.

About two hours in, we'd drank enough liquor and beer to kill a person with alcohol poisoning, but I knew my limit and my brothers'. Leaning against the wall, I tilted my long neck bottle back and gulped a few swigs. I had a nice buzz going, almost enough to make me forget about the shit from earlier tonight.

I wish things hadn't gone to hell about twenty seconds later, but life was like that.

I had the worst fuckin' luck imaginable.

My eyes flicked about the room, taking in the scene. I was always on alert. It was a hard habit to break. I'd saved my ass more than a few times by keeping a close eye on my surroundings.

The front doors swung open with force, the heavy wood banging against the solid walls and cracking with a finality that seemed like some rabid harbinger of death. I immediately recognized the guys who entered. Their cuts bore Satan's Outlaw's emblem on the leather.

"Edge," R.J. whispered, ticking his head in their direction so slightly I might have missed it if I wasn't already clued in.

"Chill, let them make the first move."

Ghost was next to me on my right only a few seconds later. R.J. stayed on my left, but his hand hovered over his shirt, ready to lift and grab his gun at the first sign of trouble. Valan and Jake kept to their game of pool. G.Q. stayed just slightly to my six, his arms around two hot blondes, one of which had been fondling his junk all night. I swear that fucker got laid ten times more than any of the rest of us, but I saw him stiffen slightly, so I knew he had seen the Outlaws too. In all outward appearance, you'd never know we were ready to rumble, but that was how that shit was supposed to look.

The following five minutes would be forever ingrained in my memory.

The seven members of the Outlaws strode forward with purpose in our direction at the exact moment the front doors of the bar opened again. Blinking, I was sure I must be imagining things because what I saw next defied logic. My beer halfway to my lips, I froze. In total disbelief and shock, I didn't move a muscle.

Are you shitting me? How is this happening? Where did she come from?

What the fuck was she doing here!?

My girl, my lost love, and most profound regret stood next to a group of girlfriends, totally oblivious to my presence or reaction and in undeniable danger.

I hadn't seen her in two years.

"Fuck," I whispered, the beer slipping through my fingers and falling to the floor with a shatter.

R.J. saw her; next, his jaw dropping open and gaping like a fish out of water. "Rae."

I couldn't tear my eyes away from her; that was my first mistake, but it wouldn't be my last. Had I been watching, I would have seen the knife that withdrew from my nemesis's hand and his quickened steps.

Since middle school, I'd been at odds with Bryce 'Killer' Hutchinson (he had a stupid name *and* nickname). We hated each other, but the roots of that hatred had much more to do with how bad we fucked with each other more than anything else.

He was a dick.

I was shoved to the side as Ghost blocked Bryce's intentional attempt to gut me with his knife. The blade sliced into Ghost's forearm but wasn't deep enough to make him pause. Without hesitating, his elbow met Bryce's chin as I snapped into action. Before I could think it through, the five of us ended up in a brawl with the seven of them.

I always liked low odds.

Maybe I was just the underdog, but I liked proving people wrong, and I enjoyed shocking them when they found out how strong and fast I was, like in the ring. Boxing had lots of perks. Not many fucked with me once they saw I could kick some serious ass, even less when they found out I was a member of the RRMC. Toss in the fact that I was intelligent and educated; I was lethal.

Right in the thick of things, throwing kicks and punches, I noticed Bryce recognize Rae, and a devilish smile curved his lips. Following his gaze, I met her startled brown irises, wide with shock.

Baby.

With that one look, so intense and heated, I knew I still owned her heart.

Tonight, she'd know she still owned mine too.

Bryce broke free of Jake's hold and ran in her direction. I wasn't sure how I made it to her before he did, but my only thought was that I had to reach her first. I moved so fast I hardly registered the motion.

There was something odd about the way my body jolted forward, but I didn't pay much attention to it. In a split-second decision, I tackled Bryce to the floor, raising my fist and punching him as hard as I could, hoping to knock him out.

While we grappled on the floor, the entire bar erupted in chaos.

Fights were breaking out among the patrons as my brothers tried not to involve any citizens, but it was near impossible. The Outlaws were brutal, using more than fists and heavily booted feet in their attacks. Sharp blades gleamed silver in the darkened bar as they caught the dim lighting. I heard a grunt and then a scream and lifted my head as one of the Outlaws grabbed Rae. A blade pressed against her slender throat.

I couldn't say what happened next.

I think I roared like a wild fucking animal and shoved through nearby bodies, using every ounce of strength I possessed to reach her, charging like a goddamn bull. Her frightened whimper increased my rage, and the feral beast inside me thirsted for fuckin' blood.

I saw red.

Nobody was going to hurt my ol' lady.

The next thing I knew, I was on the ground, the stupid fucker beneath me as I let loose. Rae was huddled with her friends, crying and calling my name, but I couldn't stop.

"Pete!"

Fuck. She was the only one that called me by my real name anymore. It nearly brought me back from the . . . *edge,* but screw this shit. She was the most important person in my life.

I had to save her. I had to make sure this fucker didn't go after her again. I had to—

"Edge!"

Jake and R.J. yanked me off the guy as I dripped his blood from my knuckles and heaved, my chest tight with the lack of oxygen. It was a wonder I didn't have a fuckin' heart attack. Pumped full of adrenaline and seething anger, I was a ticking time bomb. I fought them off, cursing and shouting, trying to run for Rae. Her doe-like brown eyes were frightened . . . of *me.*

Fuck!

The front doors burst open, and cops filed into the bar, guns drawn. Someone must have called. No doubt the presence of two rival MCs amped shit up a bit. I was shoved to the ground with the rest of my brothers and the SOMC members, as well as several rowdy citizens. Cuffed and trying to crane my head around to find my girl, I nearly panicked.

I couldn't find her.

Where the fuck was Rae?

It wasn't until I was shoved roughly into the back of a squad car that I caught a glimpse of her. Rae's slim frame was illuminated in the dark, misty night by blue and red flashing lights.

The rain had soaked her to the bone, and she was wrapped in a blanket near a few of her friends, crying and trembling, shaking her head at an officer as he indicated she should get in the waiting ambulance.

Our eyes met for a few brief seconds, and all I saw was her face pinched in pain.

My heart nearly stopped.

The words *I love you* died on my tongue as I whispered her name, and she turned away, the tears glistening on her pale cheeks. I knew at that moment that nothing I could say or do would change the way she thought of me. Her gaze spoke the words even if she never voiced them aloud.

Monster.

She was right.

I *was* a fuckin' monster. A demon, a broken man with nothing left to lose. And now I knew I was every bit the haunted and dangerous criminal I had become.

Edge.

My name and my fate.

That was where I lived and played, where I was dumped and broken, where I'd continue to stay until this life finally claimed me, and only then would I be free.

Sins of the Father, Ravage Riders MC is available now!

About the Author

Nikki Landis is the USA Today & International Bestselling, Multi-Award-Winning Author of over 50 romance novels in the MC, reverse harem, paranormal, dystopian, and science fiction genres. Her books feature deadly reapers, dark alpha heroes, protective shifters, and seductive vampires along with the feisty, independent women they love. There's heart-throbbing action on every page as well as fated mates and soul bonds deep enough to fulfill every desire.

Made in the USA
Middletown, DE
09 May 2022